# Pavi Sharma's Guide to Going Home

# PAVI SHARMA'S GUIDE TO GOING HOME

## Bridget Farr

LITTLE, BROWN AND COMPANY

New York  Boston

Copyright © 2019 by Bridget Farr

Cover art copyright © 2019 by Abigail Dela Cruz
Cover design by Marcie Lawrence
Cover copyright © 2019 by Hachette Book Group, Inc.

Little, Brown and Company
Hachette Book Group
1290 Avenue of the Americas, New York, NY 10104
Visit us at LBYR.com

First Edition: September 2019

Little, Brown and Company is a division of Hachette Book Group, Inc.
The Little, Brown name and logo are trademarks of
Hachette Book Group, Inc.

The publisher is not responsible for websites (or their content) that are
not owned by the publisher.

Library of Congress Cataloging-in-Publication Data
Names: Farr, Bridget, author.
Title: Pavi Sharma's guide to going home / by Bridget Farr.
Description: First edition. | New York ; Boston : Little, Brown and
Company, 2019. | Summary: Pavi teaches other foster children how to
navigate the system, so when she learns a young girl is being placed
with a terrible foster family, she recruits friends to help save her.
Identifiers: LCCN 2018050092| ISBN 9780316491068 (hardcover) |
ISBN 9780316491082 (ebook) | ISBN 9780316491099
(library edition ebook)
Subjects: | CYAC: Foster children—Fiction. | Helpfulness—Fiction. |
Friendship—Fiction. | Family life—Fiction.
Classification: LCC PZ7.1.F3678 Pav 2019 | DDC [Fic]—dc23
LC record available at https://lccn.loc.gov/2018050092

ISBNs: 978-0-316-49106-8 (hardcover), 978-0-316-49108-2 (ebook)

Printed in the United States of America

LSC-C

10 9 8 7 6 5 4 3 2 1

For Shiva, who found his way home

# FRONT DOOR FACE

Front Door Face. It's the perfect mix of puppy dog eyes and a lemonade stand smile, the exact combination to make the foster parents holding open their front door welcome you home. Or at least let you come inside so you don't have to stand there awkwardly while your caseworker reminds them they already signed the paperwork. They have to take you, at least for the night.

You don't want to cry—makes you seem needy. Makes them worry you'll sob all the time and maybe wet the bed they've tucked you into. Or the sleeping bag. Depends on the family.

No sneering, no glares, because then they're just picturing you tearing through the house, jumping on the couch and throwing pillows across the room. They're expecting rage from the moment they see your wrinkled lip and scrunched-up nose. I know why you're mad. And they would, too, if they knew your life. But they don't. That's why they're taking you. So don't make them regret it from the moment they see you through the screen.

But don't go overboard on the smile, either. Then you look psychotic, as if all the heartbreak in your life is just boiling under the surface, waiting to spill over and stain their new carpet. Mix it up. A little sad, but not broken down. Not happy, but with a bit of "chin up" spirit. Adults are going to tell you that all the time, so you might as well learn to do it. The sooner you get your Front Door Face down, the better.

Trust me. After four foster families and a sixty-day shelter stay, I know it works. But nobody was there to teach me the first time. It was two in the morning when they took me to my first home. I was wearing stinky pajamas and my hair was a mess, since I'd been home sick for days, my only meals Hot Cheetos and Sprite. A caseworker with tomato-red hair practically dragged me up the steps of this craggily old house, and we waited until a man with brown shoes and shaggy gray hair finally opened the door. The caseworker called me "Pave-y" Sharma, not "Puh-vi," but I was too tired to correct her, and before she could even tell him any more of my details, I threw up a bloodred mess all over his brown shoes. It wasn't my fault—I *had* the flu—but I looked like demon spawn with red spewing out of me and dripping down my chin. Definitely not a good first impression. My foster dad didn't really want to let me in after that. He did, but things could have been a lot better if I had showed up with my best Front Door Face.

For now, have yours ready. And make sure you eat something normal before you head over. Just in case. Your caseworker should have some crackers or something in her desk. They always do.

"Questions?"

Santos, the eighth grader sitting across from me, shakes his head and his dark hair flops over his even darker eyes. He's not my first eighth-grade client, but he's a little intimidating to talk to because he's so much bigger than me, and he's been scowling the whole time. But I keep going since I'm the professional here.

"Really, no questions?" I adjust my seat, since the brick ledge is starting to cut into the small part of my leg between my shorts and my knees. "I know it's a lot of information, but it's not your first family, right?"

He shakes his head, not making eye contact. One

white earbud dangles around his neck, the other hidden beneath his red hood.

"If you think of anything, write it down. Jamone, who gave you my information, can answer some questions, too. He just got his new family last month, so he remembers all of this."

I look over the rest of my list. Front Door Face. Check. Food. Check. Things to pack in your backpack. Check. School stuff. I'll wait until our next meeting for that. I move to the next letter in the outline. FFR: Foster Family Research.

"Do you know the name of your new family?"

"Alma Graves."

Spooky.

"I don't recognize the name, but give me a few days to ask around and see what I can find out. I'll google her tonight, too. When are they gonna place you?"

He shrugs. "Lenny says next week."

"I know Lenny! He's a good guy. Do you know about giving him Snickers bars when you want something?"

"Heard about it."

"It totally works. He loves Snickers. Eats them for breakfast. I once saw him dunk it in his coffee like a doughnut. Who's your caseworker?"

He shrugs. "Mary something."

"Mary Beth? The lady who laughs all the time?"

"I don't know."

I'll have to figure that out, too. I know the shelter staff better, but caseworkers make all the big calls. I won't see my caseworker, Ms. Veronica, for three more weeks, or I would see if she knows anything about Santos's caseworker.

I close my notebook and pull out the calendar I made in yearbook class. I used the library's color printer without permission, but color looks more professional than black-and-white.

"Since you move sometime next week, how about I see you next Wednesday? Right after school?"

"Yeah, all right."

He hops off the ledge and begins scanning the street in front of us like he's getting ready to bolt. He shoves his hands in his pockets before turning back to me.

"How much I owe you?"

"You don't need to pay me yet. The first meeting is always free, but have my payment ready when we meet Wednesday. I'll get a message to you if I don't find anything on your foster mom, and you won't owe me the full price. Unless you want me to do more research."

"Cool."

"Oh, and practice your Front Door Face. Use a mirror if you can."

He nods and then looks both ways before running across the street, his hands clasping the bottom straps of his backpack so it doesn't bounce on his back. I wonder where he's running to.

I carefully tuck my calendar into my work notebook, sliding both in the hot-pink backpack I've covered with Sharpie doodles of stars and moons to hide its Barbie-like hideousness. As I'm zipping it, I hear my name from behind me. It's my foster mom's son, Hamilton Jennings, ready to walk me home.

Hamilton's baritone taps against the sidewalk every few beats, marking the tempo like his very own metronome. I don't know why he picked such a big instrument when he's one of the smallest kids in seventh grade—he practically fits underneath my armpit. He says the baritone reminds him of the Macy's Thanksgiving Day Parade that he and his mom, Marjorie, went to when he was five. Since then, he's always wanted to play the tuba, but no seventh graders are allowed to. Thus, the little-brother baritone.

"Mom asked Mr. Ortman to remind us that she has parent-teacher conferences tonight," he says, his breathing heavy. "We are in charge of turning on the Crock-Pot when we get home. She says it's curry."

When Marjorie met me and found out I was Indian American, she took a cooking class to learn to make Indian food: a few types of curries, *daal*, treats like samosas and biryani. Now she makes Indian food once a week, even though I don't really remember the exact meals Ma cooked for me when I lived with her. I was pretty young then, so only certain smells are familiar. And mostly we ate a lot of sandwiches or macaroni and cheese or leftovers from the Chinese restaurant she worked at for a while. Hamilton doesn't like all the spices in Indian food, so he just eats the naan with peanut butter and jelly.

"I can't walk home with you today," I tell him as I adjust my backpack.

"Why? Are you meeting that boy again?" Hamilton sets the baritone down with a thud. "How do you even know him? Isn't he an eighth grader?"

"He is, and I just know him."

"He looks like trouble."

"He is. Sort of." For a kid in the magnet program, Santos skips a lot of his classes. I don't know how he made it to eighth grade, since he hangs out on the second-floor stairwell practically every day.

"You know we are not allowed to date until we're sixteen, right?"

I give him a look. "One, Marjorie is not my mom and therefore can't make decisions like that about my life, and two, I'm not dating him. He's just someone I know from Before."

The phrase works just like I expected. Hamilton always clams up when I talk about "Before." I don't know what he actually knows about my life before his mom took me in; probably little to nothing, which he turned into a melodramatic something. He doesn't realize that while being a foster kid can be hard, families are families and houses are houses and school is school. Before is different, and sometimes scary, but mostly it's just the past.

"Can you at least tell me where you're going?" Hamilton asks as he pushes up his red glasses. "So I can let Mom know?"

"I'm going to Crossroads to see some kids I knew when I lived there. I won't be long." If I can get the basic information I need from Lenny about Santos's foster mom then I should be able to get home quickly and do my typical Google searches. I'd like to find out what her house looks like and whether she speaks Spanish, since I know he does. Hopefully I can have his Future

Family portfolio ready to go by tomorrow. At least with preliminary information. "We can do math together when I get home."

"Okay," Hamilton says. "But be careful with that eighth grader. He looks kinda mean."

"He's not mean. He's just a foster kid, too."

Hamilton nods.

"Foster kid" works the same way as "Before."

# CROSSROADS

In the twenty minutes it takes me to walk to Cross-roads, I eat half a bag of Hot Cheetos and now have a burning stomach and red-stained fingers. I know all about the dangers of junk food and artificial flavors, but I can't stop eating them. They're tied to one of my worst memories, but also one of my best: me watching late-night television talk shows with Ma, a bowl of Hot Cheetos on the couch between us. Ma hated most junk food, but this was our special treat. I try to suck the tips of my fingers clean, since brushing them on my clothes will definitely alert Marjorie to my sneakiness. She hates junk food, just like Ma did. During my walk, I pass several bus stops full of people clasping grocery bags. I'll probably take one of these buses back, since Marjorie doesn't like me to walk in the dark.

Eventually, I come to the open field around the gray brick buildings that are Crossroads. The same overused swing set stands between the main group building and the boys' house to the left. You can't see the girls' dormitory from the street. It's surprisingly quiet, but I guess most kids are still at after-school clubs.

I open the fence, pushing hard, since the gate always gets stuck on the uneven sidewalk. I bound up the few steps to the front door and push it open. Immediately, I'm hit by the scent of Fabuloso, the lavender-scented floor cleaner the custodians always use. It was so different from the smell of my house, which always smelled like bleach. Ma loved to clean, especially on her bad days, her hands red and raw from scrubbing for hours. The sweet lavender at Crossroads was one of the only comforting changes in a world where everything was different.

"Janie? Keisha? Lenny?" I call out, noticing the empty front desk. "Where is everybody?" No one responds, but I notice a small girl sitting on one of the waiting room chairs, her legs swinging back and forth. She looks kindergarten age, maybe younger, and her deep-brown face is smudged with the chocolate from a candy bar or even an ice-cream cone, but who am I to judge with my red fingers. Her hair is pulled into a variety of small braids, brightly colored barrettes attached to each end. Tiny limbs poke out of the pink T-shirt she has on, it's so big I can't tell if she is wearing shorts underneath.

"Hey," I say.

She looks up at me with suspicion. "Hi."

"Do you know where anybody is?"

She splays her hands. "She told me to wait."

"Who told you? Janie? Keisha?" I step forward to see if I can spot anyone down the hallway.

"The lady." That was not helpful. I almost ask her if Lenny is here before remembering she doesn't know names yet. It usually takes the little ones a while to learn anyone's name.

We wait in silence for a few minutes before Janie bursts through the side office door, a stack of folders and a bucket of sidewalk chalk in her hands.

"Hey, Pav!" She reaches over the counter so she can give me a high five. Janie loves high fives. She should be a kids' soccer coach or something. "I haven't seen you in a while. Look at you now!"

What does she see? Have I changed that much from the scrawny nine-year-old with tangled black hair and pants so short you could almost see my knees? Do I look like a kid who eats three meals a day and sleeps eight hours every night and participates in clubs that have a fee? I know I'm different, but sometimes I don't feel like it. Sometimes I feel exactly the same as the day I showed up here. Tiny, smaller than the space between protons and neutrons. Almost invisible, like a dandelion seed about to be blown away. But helping kids has made me bigger.

I readjust my backpack. "Is Lenny here?"

"Yeah," she says, taking a seat again. "He was checking the boys' hall, but I'll radio him. You can wait for him in his office."

"No problem." I take one more look at the little girl waiting, wondering if I looked that small when I first got here.

In the hallway, I turn into the first office, which Lenny shares with Keisha. A pennant for the University of Texas at Austin hangs above his desk, right next to his newly framed diploma. Keisha isn't here, either, so I take a seat on the metal folding chair across from Lenny's desk. Looking at the stack of files, I'm tempted to stash one in my backpack, but I've never had to steal my information. Give Lenny enough Snickers bars, and he usually tells me what I need, even if technically he's not supposed to. I think he doesn't worry about it because he thinks, *She's a kid. What's she gonna do with the information?* He appreciates that I chat up the new kids. He thinks I'm mentoring them, which technically I am. He just doesn't know about the research or the payment in snacks and school supplies.

I'm only there a few minutes before I hear Lenny's booming voice. "Pavi Sharma. Superstar." He gives me a fist bump. "Honor roll, perfect attendance, over a year with the family. So, what's up? I haven't seen you in a couple weeks." Lenny grabs a pen from his desk and begins to twirl it, dropping it every three or four spins. Some kids leave Crossroads and never want to come back, but I need Lenny for information, and the center for clients, so I stop by at least once a month.

"School's been busy. It's progress report time, so all the teachers have us finishing projects."

"Making volcanoes! Cool."

"No volcanoes. This is a magnet program, not kindergarten. I had to take a math test, write an essay, and get three letters of recommendation to get into my school."

"I know. I wrote one. So, what is it today, Ms. Sharma?"

I scoot forward in my chair so I can lean my elbows on his desk.

"I need some background information...."

He frowns. "You know I can't give you personal information about kids at the shelter."

"Not a kid. Foster parent."

"I can't give you that information, either. You know that."

I slap a Snickers bar onto his desk.

"Are you trying to bribe me, Ms. Sharma?"

"Alma Graves. Just took in a new foster. Know her?"

"Creepy last name," he says, his twirling pen clinking into the potted cactus on his desk. "Does sound familiar, though."

"Can you look her up?"

"Pavi..."

Boom, another Snickers bar lands on his desk.

He laughs. "I can't tell you much, nothing too private, but let me look."

I wait as he types on his ancient computer.

"Okay, so..." Lenny taps the screen. "Looks like she recently got placed with one of our current Crossroads kids, though that's all I'll say about that...." He gives me a pointed look, but I focus on my notes, since I already know that information. He continues to type. "She was on the host committee for the Foster Angels Appreciation Luncheon last year. I found her on a group e-mail."

"Foster Angels? What are we, then? The Foster Fuzzies? Angel Babies?"

"I would never call you a Fuzzy."

He watches me as I take a few more notes. I wonder if she's had any previous foster kids. I'll have to check with Amber at school tomorrow. She's at Happy Hearts, one of the other shelters in Austin, and she might be able to get me some information from the kids there.

"Anything else you need? Social security number? High school transcript? Blood type?" He leans back in his office chair.

"No, this is good for now." I shove my notebook in my backpack. "Actually, can I use your computer to print something?" Marjorie's printer is out of paper, and I need more forms for my introduction meetings. I used my last one with Santos.

"No problem. Just give me a second to close some things."

I look around the office while he types. "Who's the girl in the lobby? Is she new?"

Lenny tears open one of the Snickers bars. "Meridee? She's been here, what? Twelve days or so? Won't be here long because I think they got her a placement already."

"Wow, that's good for her." There aren't enough

foster families, so it's hard for anyone to get a placement that fast, but it's especially hard to find forever families for black and brown kids like Meridee, Santos, and me.

"Is this her first time in the shelter?"

"I think so. At least her first time at Crossroads."

For a moment, I think about all the reasons she could have ended up here, but I know I'll never ask. In my job, I can't fix people's families. I can only focus on the future.

Normally I don't take clients so young, and I definitely won't make her pay, but she is even younger than I was when I went into foster care, and something about her ginormous T-shirt and dirty face makes me want to help. I don't want her to feel alone like I did the first time.

Lenny flips through a stack of folders on his desk before pushing back his rolling chair.

"All yours."

"Thanks. It should only take five minutes."

Once he's out the door, I quickly log in to my online school account. I consider printing multiple copies of my forms to update my folders, but then notice that Lenny's printer is almost empty, too. As I'm closing out of my e-mail, I bump the tab for a page Lenny accidentally left open. It must be the database they use for the foster kids, because it lists the little girl's name (Meridee Grant) and her birthdate, intake date, etc. Man, my job would be so much easier if I had access to this.

Then I see it.

Temporary placement.

George and Janet Nickerson.

I almost vomit red Cheetos all over the floor. Again.

# THE NICKERSONS

It was his brown shoes I threw up on that first night with the redheaded social worker and me with the flu and no home anymore. True, I had a house still, but it hadn't been a home in a long time. So here I was at this gloomy house with this tall man and his mop of gray hair that drooped into his eyes so I couldn't really see him. The caseworker shrieked when she saw the vomit, but Mr. Nickerson didn't flinch. Since I couldn't see his eyes, I couldn't tell if he was looking down at the mess or at my face. I was too tired to be horrified at what I had done. I felt relieved, actually, feeling a little bit better. I guess I needed that.

"I am so sorry, Mr. Nickerson!" the redhead exclaimed. "Let me see if I have something for you."

She began digging in her huge black bag, pushing around papers and pens while she searched for a tissue or a used napkin that had been wrapped around her breakfast. Mr. Nickerson shook his foot so the red slime slid onto the porch.

"I got something inside."

She looked from him to me. "This wasn't how I was hoping to make this introduction, but Mr. Nickerson, this is Pavi Sharma."

"She sick or something?" He rubbed the stubble on his pale chin.

"I don't know." She looked at me. "Are you sick, sweetie?"

I couldn't speak. The days of lying on the couch watching talk shows with an empty garbage can and bottles of Sprite by my side seemed like years ago. Was I sick? I didn't know. If she asked my name, I wouldn't have been able to answer.

The redhead put her hand on my back. "She's probably just a bit nervous. Is Mrs. Nickerson here?"

"She's sleeping. It's two o'clock in the morning."

Bugs swarmed near the porch light, none flying

toward the open door and Mr. Nickerson's face. Even they didn't want to go inside.

"We sure are grateful you'll be taking Pavi. She's a sweet girl. She'll be here for a few days as part of her emergency stay, but I know you two have been considering long-term placement."

I don't remember the rest of what she said, but I know there was talk of phone calls and dates, and then she was hugging me—I wished it was Ma hugging me—and then she pushed me toward Mr. Nickerson and the gloom behind the metal screen door.

～

"Pavi? Pavi? Are you okay?" Lenny's voice guides me like a lighthouse from my memories. He's standing across from me, one hand on the desk like a sprinter at the starting line, the other reached out toward me. I wonder if he thought I might fall out of the chair. I stay frozen in place, needing a moment before I stand up. I want to get away from this place and those names. I want to be home where I can let the sound of Hamilton's baritone shoo away thoughts of the two worst people I've ever met.

"I'm fine....I just got..." I stop, because I don't know

what to say. I got shocked with memories? Punched by the past?

"You look like you saw a ghost. Here." He hands me one of the unopened Snickers bars. "Maybe your blood sugar is low?"

I shove the candy in my back pocket, feeling like a zombie just woken from the dead. Then it hits me.

"Lenny, you can't send her there."

"Send who where?"

"That little girl. Meridee. You can't send her to her new placement."

He frowns, looking confused. "Why?"

"I accidentally saw the name of the family she's going to on your computer...."

Lenny sighs. "I thought I closed that all out."

"I wasn't snooping, but I know them, Lenny! Her new family, and she can't go there." I stumble over my words as I race to get them out. "It's not good, Lenny. She won't—"

"Slow down. I can barely understand you. What happened?"

I'm afraid to say it. From the back of my memory comes the barking, the sounds of chains clanging.

"They have all these dogs, and sometimes...they fight."

Lenny rubs a hand across his chin, his eyebrows raised. "They had dogfights?"

"Yes."

"How old were you when you stayed with them?"

"Nine." I can see the doubt on his face. "But I remember!"

Lenny perches on the edge of his desk, his palms pressed together in his lap. "I'm not saying you're wrong, but you were pretty young, so those dogs probably seemed scary. Like they were fighting. The family has been evaluated. They've been verified."

I shake my head. "I'm not exaggerating. I know what happened. Can't you just keep her at Crossroads until her caseworker can check them out again?"

Lenny shakes his head. "We're already over capacity, and she has a placement. She's going to be okay, Pav. You need to just let the adults take care of it."

Adults have caused all the problems I've ever had. "Please, just a day..."

His cell phone rings, and he pulls it out of his back pocket. He sighs when he sees it. "Not again."

I stand up, knowing I'm about to miss my chance. "Please, Lenny."

"It's gonna be okay, Pav. I'm glad you care so much. I'll call and check in with her caseworker if it will make you feel better. You can chill here for a bit if you want, but I gotta run."

He's out the door, answering his phone before he can even finish his sentence. I swipe my backpack from the floor, the sounds of a kid shouting starting to fill the hall.

When I enter the lobby, Meridee is still alone in the waiting room, but now there's a stack of books on the chair beside her. She has one in her lap, her fingers slowly turning the pages as she mouths a story I can't understand. I crouch down beside her.

"Hi, Meridee. I'm Pavi."

"Puffy?"

"No. Pavi. Puh. Vee."

She shrugs her shoulders before flipping another page in her book. I want to make her disappear, to stash her in Neverland or up in Rapunzel's castle. I don't know how much time I have to make a miracle, but I have to try.

"Do you like Hot Cheetos? You can have the rest." I hand her the half-eaten bag, feeling a bit guilty I don't have anything to offer besides junk food. I'll do better when I come next time. She doesn't eat any, but tucks the bag between her back and the chair.

"I gotta go now...."

I take a step back from her, knowing I'm the only one who can keep her safe.

~

When I finally make it home, I see Hamilton through the front window. He's sitting at the counter, his head bent over what I assume is our math homework. It's getting dark, so I know Marjorie will be worried, reconsidering her decision not to buy Hamilton and me cell phones until we're eighth graders. If I had one, I know it would be vibrating like crazy, filling up with her five *W* questions: Where are you? What are you doing? Who are you with? When will you be home? Why didn't you tell me about this earlier? Marjorie crosses back and forth behind the window, moving between the dishwasher and the cupboards. She wipes back a blonde curl before rubbing her hands on her favorite floral apron.

Life is so easy for them. It's like all those kids who have birthday parties every year; they don't know what it's like not to have anyone around to sing over the candles. And it's not that I want Hamilton to know. I don't want him to worry about where he's going to sleep at night or what he's going to eat for dinner. But tonight, I wish they knew a little. I trudge up the steps and the door opens before I even grab the handle.

"Pavi! Where have you been? It's dark!" Marjorie's eyes are wide as she pulls me into her arms, and I take a deep inhale of her rose-scented perfume mixed with a hint of garlic. I'm folded into her cozy sides, her damp apron pressed against my cheek.

"Sorry I'm late."

"You are just in time! Hamilton is going to set the table." She takes off my backpack and steers me like a sailboat to the kitchen that smells even stronger of garlic and…cinnamon? The smell of the curry is familiar, touching a memory I can't quite place. For a moment, Ma's face flashes in my mind, and I push it aside.

"Too bad you didn't have a cell phone. You could have called," Hamilton says, shooting a look at Marjorie, who is biting her lip and appears to be considering the truth of that statement.

"I'm not feeling so good," I say as I back toward the entryway and the stairs that will lead to my room. I realize I don't have the energy to be a part of this happy family right now. "I think I'll go straight to bed."

"Oh, sorry, sweetie," Marjorie says as she plops the back of her palm on my forehead. "You do feel kind of hot. You go get ready for bed, and I'll bring you some tea."

"Sorry I couldn't do math with you, Hamilton. We can work on it tomorrow after school?"

"Anytime, pal," Hamilton says. "We'll get it done."

Marjorie gives me one more hug before I head up to my room. Normally I would need tonight to research on her computer, but Santos's case is pushed aside for a minute. And I don't need Google for my first step in Meridee's case, anyway. I'll never forget 702 Lovely Lane.

# PIPER AND DAVY CROCKETT

"Davy Crockett…pocket…locket…rocket!"

"Rocket?" I ask the freckled girl sitting between me and Hamilton. We're only fifteen minutes into seventh period, Texas history, and I'm ready to be out of this class. "A rocket doesn't have anything to do with Davy Crockett. They didn't even have electricity."

"Do you have a better idea?" says Piper, her hands flying to her hips, her balm-stained lips forming a perfect pout.

"I do, actually." I sing as flatly as possible, "Davy, Davy, Davy Crockett was so very patriotic."

"'Patriotic' doesn't rhyme with Crockett." She turns to Hamilton. "Right? It doesn't even rhyme."

I sigh as I write down my perfect line. "It's close enough. Right?"

I lean forward to make eye contact with Hamilton, who is staring at our practically empty lyric paper. We've been working on these Texas Heroes lyrics for two days and have barely finished a single stanza because of all the arguing. Hamilton hates getting in between Piper and me. He and Piper have been friends since before they were born. Piper's dad teaches the same grade as Marjorie, so they shared a baby shower. They take every first-day-of-school picture together, and then I got added beside Hamilton, and now Piper's smile looks a little fake.

I like Piper. Okay. That's not true. I don't like her, but I don't dislike her. She just doesn't get me. I freak her out. She sees me as a red Kool-Aid stain on her favorite dress. She had this perfect two-dom friendship with Hamilton and now there's me. He and I do homework together at home, so he doesn't go to her house as often to finish it with her. Whenever they go bowling or to ride their bikes, Marjorie always invites me along. I don't go most of the time (who wants to be the third wheel who got invited by the mom?), but sometimes I can't pass up a trip to the water park or for frozen yogurt.

Mostly, I think Piper is afraid of me. Afraid that being a foster kid is contagious and if she gets too close, her dad will suddenly stop showing up in the after-school pickup line. Every day, I remind her of the possibility that her perfect life could suddenly disappear.

And Piper doesn't like that I'm competition. We're all part of the International Studies magnet program at our public school, which means everyone had to apply to attend. She and Hamilton used to be the top kids in every class. Now I'm in the running, too, answering questions and getting As on tests.

"Seriously, Hamilton, you need to break the tie or we're never going to get this done." I lean forward so I can wave my hand in front of his face. "Hamilton!"

Just as his head starts to lift, Mr. Ramirez's timer begins to chime. "Okay, ladies and gentlemen, time to pack up. Final lyrics must be submitted tomorrow so you're ready to practice with the music. Please put any finished papers in the bin, and if you borrowed a pencil, turn it in. I need ten pencils back in this jar before you leave. Go!"

Hamilton pushes his chair back, and Piper scoops up all the papers and places them into a yellow folder with her name emblazoned in sparkly stickers. "I'll be in charge of these."

*Go for it*, I think as I collect Mr. Ramirez's pencils. They all have flowers taped to the top so we don't try to steal them. "Here, I'll take yours." I scoop up Hamilton's pencil with a giant daisy stuck to the top.

"Thanks." The first words he has muttered in ten minutes. I don't know why we all keep trying to work together. It's never fun. I could find a new partner, go work with Jamiya, who always does A-plus work, or Marisol, who is a little hyper but gets a lot done. Teachers often pair me with Jaya, the only other Indian American girl at school, but I always end up embarrassed when everyone expects us to be experts on India. Jaya's visited India with her grandparents; she knows the exact towns they're from and even brought pictures to show the class after her last trip. She always wears a delicate gold bracelet she got from her grandma last year, and then there's me, not knowing any of the answers to their questions. So I stick with Hamilton, the convenient partner, since we never have to finish in class; we can take whatever we need home. Really, it's Piper who should find another group.

Mr. Ramirez pats my shoulder as he counts the returned pencils. He has a small bouquet collected below his matching purple bow tie. "Eight! I need two more, people! No one's leaving until there are ten back in this jar."

When I return to our table to get my backpack, Piper is making a plan with Hamilton.

"Let's just finish it tonight so we're done. You can come over to my house right after school. Dad says he can order pizza after his meeting, so maybe your mom can come over and eat with us. We'll do it right away and still have some time to make a video."

Piper has her own YouTube channel. She shoots videos of herself doing makeup tutorials and DIY crafts that she copies from someone else's Instagram.

"Yeah, maybe, if I can use your phone to text my mom. Pavi, what do you think? Do you want to walk to Piper's after school? Then we can do math when we get home?"

"I can't right after school," I say as I push my chair in and move toward the back of the line to leave.

"Why?" Hamilton asks.

"I have some stuff to do."

"What? What do you have to do?"

"Just things."

Hamilton frowns. "Are you meeting that eighth grader again?"

"Why are you being so nosy?"

"Why are you being so secretive? Are you going out with him or something?"

"You are far too young to have a boyfriend," Piper says, her hands back on her hips. "We are not developmentally ready."

"Maybe *you're* not," I say before turning to Hamilton. "He's not my boyfriend. Remember, I'm going to Crossroads?" I don't normally lie, but I can't tell him I'm going to the Nickersons'. He'd freak if he knew I was headed to the "bad" part of town. Kids like Hamilton and Piper, who have only lived in one type of neighborhood, often judge the people living in other ones. My favorite family before Marjorie lived with five kids and their *abuela* in the "bad" part of a town. My second-to-worst family had a pool in their backyard and a woman to clean their house every Monday. Money doesn't make a good family. Love does that.

"Oh, right," he says, instantly backing down, though I hear him mutter, "Why didn't you just say that?"

The bell rings, and Piper pauses at the door, blocking me in.

"Hamilton and I will take care of the poem. We'll rock it, just like Davy Crockett!" She beams at her own poetry. "And since Hamilton and I are writing the lyrics, it seems only fair that you type them up and e-mail them back to me."

"I can do that."

"You know Mr. Ramirez's rules? Black. Twelve-point font. And only Times New Roman or Arial."

"Got it," I say, now really considering making a red-rover-style attack and getting out of here. "I do know how to use a computer, Piper."

She gives me a look that suggests she doesn't agree. "You haven't taken keyboarding yet."

"Don't worry," Hamilton argues. "Pavi's really good with the computer. She is a crazy-fast typist."

Piper frowns, clearly hoping he was on her side. I've had enough.

"I have things to do tonight, Piper, other than having you review my keyboarding skills. I'll have it to you tomorrow. Hot-pink font."

"Wait! No!" she says, her eyes wide before she sees Hamilton laughing and realizes I'm kidding. "Just get it done. *Right.*"

Finally safe in the hallway, I check the clock and realize I have only eight minutes to get to the bus stop. I start to walk faster when I hear Hamilton calling my name.

"Are you really going to Crossroads?" he says, breathless when he catches up to me. I continue to power walk down the stairs and toward the side exit of the building.

"I'm going to Crossroads."

"Weren't you there yesterday? You're going two days in a row?"

"Yes. A friend is moving out soon, and I want to see her before she goes and I never do again."

"You sure you're not meeting the eighth grader? It's okay if you are. You can tell me."

"I'm going to Crossroads, and if I don't run I'm going to miss my bus."

Hamilton pushes up his glasses, which have inched down his nose. "Okay...well, thanks for typing the lyrics. Then we can finish that math homework from yesterday?"

"Sure. Fine. I gotta run, Hamilton. Tell Marjorie I'll be home before dark."

I take off running before I can hear his response.

# GOING TO THE NICKERSONS'

I get off the bus at the local grocery store. The stop is full of people with worn faces, overflowing plastic bags propped next to their feet. The construction guys' bags must be full of the bits of their uneaten lunches and the button-down shirts they wore to work but now can't stand in the heat. A few moms sit with their kids on their laps. There are a few homeless men, one standing with his head resting against the glass, the other sitting on the cement sidewalk with his back to the bench. The old woman beside him doesn't mind his head resting on the side of her knee.

I scan the bus stop, knowing the Nickersons probably aren't here, but wanting to be careful anyway. This is their part of town. If they still live here. They might have moved. That's what I'm investigating. Their neighborhood looks almost the same as the one I grew up in, but here, people have houses instead of apartments. Not fancy houses, but still—houses.

Out of my backpack I pull a baseball cap from Hamilton's Little League days and a pair of binoculars from when he was in Boy Scouts. I attempt to pull the cap low over my eyes, but it's not much of a disguise. I doubt they had many foster kids who looked like me.

I strap the binoculars around my neck and take off down the sidewalk.

The streets are empty as I make the ten blocks to Lovely Lane. Sweat is starting to accumulate under my backpack. I stay on the opposite side of the road, trying to keep behind cars and trucks as much as possible. I pause when I'm across from Ms. Bell's bright-pink house; I miss sitting on her porch and eating her sugar-free candies. I used to wish she would adopt me. That was back in the days when I had big hope, fairy-tale hope, the kind of hope that makes you believe that if you just gathered enough balloons, you could really grab on and float into the sky.

For a long time, I hoped my mom would change. That she'd show up with her face clean and her clothes ironed, her once-vacant eyes actually seeing me again, and she'd take my hand, and we'd walk out the door together. Then, I hoped Ms. Bell would adopt me. Or my first-grade teacher, Mr. Kim. Then the bus driver or the woman I saw walking dogs near our elementary school.

Soon, my hopes got smaller. I hoped that I could stay one night with Ms. Bell, maybe for my birthday or a holiday. I hoped for the dogs to stop barking, to stop getting sent to the school counselor for a change of clothes, since mine hadn't been washed all week. My hopes got so small that I couldn't see them, even though I knew they weren't gone.

But that hope has come back, started to return like flowers in spring. It's not a rose garden of hope, not even a large bloom, but a bud, pushing its way through years of dirt. I don't hope Meridee's mom will get better. I don't hope she gets a perfect family. It's a small hope, a growing hope that has led me to the sidewalk outside a door I promised I would never again enter. Suddenly I hear the sound I was hoping, stupidly hoping, didn't exist anymore.

Dogs. Vicious, barking dogs mixed with the whine of small ones that are hungry or lonely or too young to have been taken from their mothers. I hide behind a black Suburban across from the house with a cracked porch light and a white screen door that doesn't sit quite straight. I crouch down beside the wheel, knowing I can pretend to tie my shoe if anyone comes by. The red pickup truck I was looking for isn't in the driveway. If they still live here, Mrs. Nickerson will be home, but she'll be in her room with the TV blasting. Even if she did hear me, she would never come to the door. She never even leaves her bedroom.

Thankfully, there is a FOR SALE sign in the front yard of the neighbor's house, and from the look of it, no one has lived there for a while. I crawl around the front of the Suburban so I can inspect the backyard with my binoculars, but all I can see are the neighbor's overgrown weeds and the big wooden fence. I'll have to go back there and look myself.

My heart pounding, I race across the street to the neighbor's yard, hiding behind the side bushes separating the houses. I stay close to the hedge that turns into the wooden fence a couple of feet taller than my head. The shuffling of the dogs increases, and I can hear them clanging against their metal cages. I wonder if I will recognize any of them. Would they recognize me?

Safely hidden in the backyard, I set my backpack down on the ground. The fence has two ledges, one for my feet and one for my hands, so I can look over, though I know from the sound and the smell what I'm going to see. The dogs sense someone nearby, and the barking is so loud that I can barely hear myself think. I don't worry someone will come out and yell at them, because they do this all the time. A cat, a piece of garbage blowing in the wind. I carefully put one hand on the fence, and it sways. Not giving up, I put one foot on the bottom rung. I take a deep breath, the barking filling my ears, and I use the little arm strength I have to pull myself up. Beyond the fence is the row of cages full of dogs I can't recognize from here, and the same worn circle of grass in the center of the lawn, and suddenly I'm taken back three years, to a memory I've always wanted to forget....

I was used to the barking. I knew the voice of each dog, shuddered at the calls that reached out to me from their metal cages when I dropped old, sometimes moldy dog food into their bowls. I would never have reached out to touch one, but in the daylight, they were still dogs. Sometimes they played with their bowls or dropped their tongues through the fence, slobbering the edge of my fingers or the back of my legs. During the day they were dogs, but on certain nights, fight nights, they became monsters.

One night was different. I woke up to the barks while I lay on the plastic-covered mattress, the rhythms of growls to yips to whines so familiar, but something was off. Still groggy, I struggled to recognize a sound inside the rumble. Then I noticed the empty spot at the end of my mattress. It was Lucky.

Lucky was my puppy as much as anything can really be yours when you're living in someone else's house, eating someone else's food. One of the dogs had a litter a few weeks earlier, and Mr. Nickerson had sold most of them within the week; they seemed too small to be taken from their mother, but I didn't know anything about dogs then. Didn't know anything about life.

No one wanted Lucky. She was small, with a slightly deformed back paw. It didn't stop her from rolling around with her brothers and sisters, but she ate less, since she couldn't get to the bowl as fast.

"She's a runt," Mr. Nickerson told me when he saw me running with her around the front lawn, her body flopping onto the browned grass when her feet couldn't keep up with her joy. "No use bothering with a runt."

But she licked my nose and snuggled me at night when we both laid beneath the threadbare sheets. In a house where I felt like a ghost, passing through the rooms unnoticed, she was someone who loved me. Someone who waited for me at the door after school when no one else would. Someone I could talk to. She wasn't perfect, but neither was the person I loved most.

Lucky wasn't in my bed that night when I woke up to the barking, and I whispered her name, pausing to check under my bed. I hoped to find her curled up in a pile of my dirty clothes the way she'd be when I got home from school, her nose tucked in a sleeve.

She must have escaped to the backyard through the screen door that never quite closed.

I snuck out the front door and headed around the side of the house. I pushed through the crowds of dirty jeans and work boots, everyone too focused on the dogs to notice me. I pushed my way up to the back step, hidden in the shadows of the work lamp that lit up the backyard.

That's when I saw her, Lucky, hobbling near the edge of the ring, an enormous pit bull with scarred jowls pulling at its chain as she hopped around it.

*She's playing*, I thought as her hind legs moved from side to side, her growl barely audible over the crowd. She loved the other dogs.

"Little dog wants to be a fighter," someone shouted, his mouth open in a booming laugh.

"She can't fight; look at that bum leg." Another voice, this one I couldn't place.

"Let's see what she can do!" another said, laughing. I scanned the crowd for Mr. Nickerson, knowing he couldn't let this happen, wouldn't let this happen, but I couldn't find him among the faces. Where was he? This was his show; he had to be close.

Then the first man leaned down beside Lucky, picking her up and holding her close to his face, her legs whirling as she squirmed. Her small tongue reached out to lick his nose. With Lucky clutched between his hands, he neared the pit bull, holding her in front of its chomping jaws.

"You wanna fight this big guy? Think you can take him?"

He grabbed her paw with one hand, giving the pit bull a swat on the nose.

"Put her down," I screamed, but no one heard me over the growing barks. Mr. Nickerson led a new dog out from one of the back kennels, and I breathed a sigh of relief. He would get her back. He knew Lucky was mine.

But he didn't notice the men as he went about tying up the second dog. He fiddled with chains and locks, pausing to whisper to a man with a microphone beside him.

"Next up, Killer and Macho…," the announcer started, and the crowd turned. The man laughed as he set Lucky down.

It happened so fast.

A growl. A yelp.

Only I saw the tiny dog with the curled foot lying motionless on the dirt.

"Oh geez, what happened?" Mr. Nickerson sighed when he noticed her. He gently picked her up, cradling her in his arms, and walked toward the back fence. "I'll be right back."

I raced toward the alley, not wanting Mr. Nickerson to know I had snuck outside, but needing to see Lucky, still hoping she would be okay.

She wasn't.

～

My arms scratch against the fence when I sway, and suddenly I am back in the present. The fence leans under my weight, and I scream as I begin to lose my footing.

And then someone grabs my shirt and pulls me to the ground.

I look up to see Hamilton standing over me, looking both confused and horrified.

"What are you doing here?" I whisper, though you couldn't hear a yell over the racket happening next door. "Aren't you supposed to be at Piper's?"

"What are you doing? With my binoculars? And my hat? Are you trying to rob this house?"

"What?" I shout, dusting the grass off my back. "I'm not robbing anybody."

"Is this your boyfriend's house, then? Is this where the eighth grader lives?"

"Your first thought was robbery and *then* that I'm seeing a boy? You are nuts!"

Hamilton shrugs. "Well, I thought you were going to see your boyfriend...."

"You followed me?"

"Obviously. Stop interrupting! You were acting so strange after school that I canceled on Piper so I could follow you. I thought I was going to catch a romantic rendezvous, but then you didn't go to the front door like a normal person, you snuck back here and then you were climbing the fence, and I realized I had to stop you before you started your life of crime!"

"Why would I rob a house like this? Don't you hear the dogs? Climbing over the fence would get my leg bitten off."

Hamilton huffs, now pacing along the side of the fence. "It was a working theory! I only had time to make observations and think of interesting questions and formulate a hypothesis! I did not get to developing testable predictions or gathering data before I had to make a decision to save you!"

I roll my eyes. "Wow, Ms. Olson would be so proud of your use of the scientific method."

"This place is creepy. And smells bad. So you need to tell me what you are doing here."

Hamilton's face is red, and the look in his eyes tells me he's not kidding. I don't know what to tell him. What I want to tell him. I've kept my business from him, from everyone, but right now, with this house from my past screaming into my future, I realize I don't want to go back there alone.

"Okay. I'll tell you. But I'll have to do it on the way home because we need to get out of here."

The red pickup truck has just pulled into the driveway.

# HAMILTON'S IN

"Let me get this straight," Hamilton says as we sit together on the bus, scrunched between two moms, their toddlers, and grocery bags. "You run a detective slash spy agency...?"

"More of a consulting business with a bit of private detective work thrown in," I explain.

"I'll come back to that detail later....So, you work for other foster kids to help them...." He pauses, raising an eyebrow.

"To help them adjust to a new home. I do some background research on families, but generally that's all done online. Climbing fences is not a normal part of the job. I also help with first meets, new houses, relationships between them and any other kids who live there, foster or biological.…"

"Am I in your brochure?" Hamilton asks with an excited smile.

"Brochures are so old. And no, you're not, but you're not a regular Bio Kid. What we have is special." I add lots of syrup to my smile, and Hamilton laughs.

"Special, indeed. You do all of this work for other foster kids and they pay you in school supplies and Hot Cheetos?"

I nod.

"I wondered how you got all those new Sharpies! And Ticonderogas!"

I flash a what-can-I-say smile, still grateful that I never again have to be the kid showing up with an empty backpack and having to ask the teacher for supplies. I push the button for our stop, knowing we better run to our house because Marjorie will be mad we're late, me for the second night in a row. We'll have to think of a cover for Hamilton.

As we rush, Hamilton asks about the Nickersons. "And today you were at the house in Creepsville because…"

"I was doing research."

"Research involves you breaking and entering?"

"Technically it would have been climbing and observing, but yes, in this case, it does."

Hamilton frowns. "So you don't normally spy into people's backyards?"

"No. Usually I can do all my research online. Or at Crossroads."

"What makes this case special?" Hamilton asks.

"There's this kid...and she's going to a really bad home, like the worst possible home, and so I'm doing what I can to keep her out of there."

"Okay...," Hamilton says as we run past our neighbors who are setting out their garbage bins for tomorrow's pickup. "How bad? Like horror-movie bad? Are they...killers?"

I frown, refusing to fulfill his need for drama. He must notice the look on my face because he immediately apologizes. We make it to the sidewalk of our house and under our tulip flag. The front drapes are closed, so we have a few minutes before Marjorie sees us and the flood of questions begins.

"I wanna help," Hamilton says as he searches for his key. Mine is already in my hand.

"Thank you, but I don't need your help."

"Why not? I'm very sleuth-y! I followed you for over an hour and you didn't even notice me until I was standing above you like a ninja."

He's right; I did have my guard down today. I'll be more careful from now on.

"This isn't your thing, Hamilton. You have baritone practice and math homework and plans to Rollerblade with Piper."

"I don't even own Rollerblades," he says as he steps in front of the door.

"Seriously, I appreciate the offer, but I got it."

I reach my hand toward the door, and he stops it.

"But you don't have to do it by yourself. I can help. That's what brothers are for."

I look at his eager face, his eyes full of hope, and I know why I don't want him to be a part of it: He doesn't know what my world looks like. He thinks kids without parents are all singing songs like Annie before they run off to meet their Daddy Warbucks. I get why he would think that; he's only ever seen his mom go to a couple of meetings before coming home with this quiet girl, but I had gotten all my crazy out before he met me. I never told him about any of the darkness Before. He thinks my worst problem is that I don't have a copy of my birth certificate.

If he goes with me, if he starts to see what life is like for those of us whose parents don't put notes in our lunch boxes, then he won't be so Hamilton-y anymore. I like that he doesn't know. That there is someone out there who gets to believe in happy families.

But I don't think I can do this alone. It's too big. I can handle the Front Door Face speech and the Google research, but I don't know if I can save Meridee on my own, and she really needs a rescue.

"Please, Pavi," Hamilton urges, his hand squeezing my wrist. "Let me help."

"Fine," I say as I push past him. "Meet me in my room after Marjorie goes to watch the news. I'll fill you in on the plan."

"Yes!" Hamilton shouts as he punches the air in triumph.

"You two get in here," Marjorie yells through the closed door.

"But it's just this once," I remind him. I need his help on this case, but after that, I'll go back to how I do things best. Alone.

~

"Stop playing with those," I tell Hamilton later that night as he sits in the center of my floor, flipping through my folders of work materials. I'm sitting on my bed with Meridee's empty case file. I don't need to research this family. I already know all the sickening details: lonely nights, unwashed clothes, and, of course, the dogs. "We only have fifteen minutes before Marjorie comes to check on us, and you didn't brush your teeth before you came over here. We also didn't finish Ms. Hulsman's math assignment, and that's due tomorrow."

"It can be late. It's only five points for daily homework."

"Fine, but you still need to focus."

I scan my brainstorming notes in my journal, and when I look up, Hamilton is sitting cross-legged in front of me, holding his own leather-bound notebook and a tiny golf pencil.

"What are you doing?"

"I'm taking notes."

"I take notes. You're here to listen."

"But I learned speed-writing shorthand the last six weeks in journalism." He holds out his notebook toward me, and it's all a bunch of scribbles that look a bit like cursive.

"That's just gibberish."

"No! It's very fast! It's only missing vowels and has abbreviations for some common words, like *v* means 'of,' 'have,' or 'very.' I can write eighty words a minute now."

"But I don't need you to take notes. I already have the notes." I show him my full journal.

"It helps me learn. I'm a visual learner."

"Whatever. Can I just start?"

He nods thoughtfully.

"Right now, there are two parts to the plan. One, make sure the right people know how bad this family is, and two, find Meridee a new home...."

"That's her name?" Hamilton asks, looking up from his notepad.

"Yeah."

He nods, adding to his strange, swirling notes. I continue.

"The first step, then, is making a report to the police or Child Protective Services about the family."

Hamilton raises his hand.

"Why are you raising your hand?"

He shrugs. "Habit."

"Well, what?"

"While I did note the house was awfully creepy with all those barking dogs, do we have a reason to not like this family other than that? You said they were bad, but do you *know* know or do you just think you know?"

"I know."

"But you're not going to tell me what you know?"

"No. And stop saying 'know' so many times."

"Done. I trust you, Detective. What's step number two?"

I stretch my neck from side to side. "I need to get back to Crossroads to see if Lenny knows any families who might be willing to take in Meridee. I'd ask my caseworker, but she's new and I won't see her for a few weeks. They're probably looking for a family connection now. Meridee's mom might even be fighting for her."

Ma fought for me. For as long as she could. I shake away the memory.

"But we're not at that step yet. It doesn't matter if there is another foster family willing to take her in as long as she's assigned to the Nickersons."

Hamilton scratches a few more notes before raising his hand again.

"You don't need to do that."

He drops it to his side. "Right. How are you going to make the call?"

"I'm not going to make it. Adults don't believe kids." My heartbeat speeds up as I remember Lenny telling me to let it go. He didn't believe me, and he knows me. No way CPS will believe some random kid. "We need someone who sounds like an adult, and I know someone who will be perfect."

Suddenly, we both freeze. Our nighttime lullaby is beginning fifteen minutes early. The first note: the click of the front door lock followed by a turn of the handle to confirm. We listen to the footsteps crossing to the kitchen, the creak of the kitchen cabinet, the beep of one minute on the microwave. We have one minute before Marjorie's cup of tea will be reheated, and she'll be on her way up the stairs to poke her head in our rooms.

"Quick!" Hamilton whispers as he begins to swipe the papers lying on the floor into a hodgepodge pile.

"Stop! You're just messing things up!"

He leaps to the door, pressing his ear against it. I get off the bed and quickly tuck the papers into the correct folders before sliding them into my bottom drawer. I meet him at the door.

"Maybe I should hide under the bed!"

I roll my eyes. "Just go! Walk fast and if you hear her on the stairs, step into the bathroom."

"Roger that."

The door creaks open. He peeks out, looking both ways before I give him a shove.

"We'll talk in the morning!" he whispers through the door.

"Go!"

Back in my bed, I quickly flick off my light and snuggle under my covers. Even with all his annoying hand-raising and weird note-taking, I realize it's better to plan with someone else, and I'm glad Hamilton is going to help. I smile as I wait for Marjorie to check on me, knowing she'll be here in a moment to see if I'm asleep.

# SOMETHING FORGOTTEN

The next morning, I spot Piper through the car window as she waits for us by the flagpole. She's wearing a plaid skirt and a white collared shirt as if she belongs to a fancy prep school. Instead of her regular backpack, she's holding a black briefcase, and in her other hand, a seedling plant in the bottom of a cut-off plastic soda bottle.

Hamilton bounds out of the car before I can warn him, kissing Marjorie through the driver's side window.

"Don't forget to bring down your laundry after school and sort it. I'll run loads when I get home," Marjorie instructs us both. "And only three piles, Hambone: lights, darks, and colors. Nothing more."

Last week, Hamilton sorted his clothes into sixteen different piles based on color, fabric, and age. Some piles contained a single item.

"Have a great day, you two. Be learners!"

After I wave good-bye, I slink over to where Piper is waiting with a tight-lipped smile. Unlike me, Hamilton doesn't remember what we forgot.

"Hey, Pipe!" Hamilton calls as he walks up to her.

"I'm assuming you brought the typed lyrics with you, since Hamilton said you guys would finish them and e-mail them to me last night." Her eyes drill into me over Hamilton's shoulder. I can tell by the way he freezes that he is just now realizing what I remembered the moment I spotted her face: In the middle of yesterday's craziness, we forgot to finish the lyrics.

"Mom's printer broke, so we are going to print it in the library," Hamilton lies before I can even jump in. "We're going to do it at lunch."

I'm surprised he looks so relaxed.

"I'm going to get us a pass from Mr. Ramirez this morning," I add.

Piper looks from him to me, trying to decide if she believes us. After a few seconds, she picks up her briefcase.

"You better have it done by seventh period."

She turns on her heel and marches through the front door. Hamilton looks over at me, guilt covering every inch of his face. I don't think he's ever forgotten an assignment, especially not a project worth such a large part of his grade, but then a tiny smile reveals his pride in his little lie.

"Meet me in the library at lunch. We'll get it done." I push him toward the door. He nods before taking off after Piper.

Alone, I wait for the morning bell.

~

During lunch, Hamilton and I sit at one of the library computers, our trays across the room on a table by the door.

"Raccoon hat with *buttons* he wore? I'm pretty sure raccoon hats don't have buttons. Give me that," I say as I reach for the lyrics Hamilton is holding an inch from his nose.

"It's not my fault I can't read Piper's attempt at cursive!"

"Just let me look at it! We're running out of time! We only have ten minutes left, and I would actually like to eat some of my lunch."

"Fine," Hamilton says as he thrusts the paper toward

me. He's right: Piper's handwriting is incredibly hard to read. The loops and curves of her letters look like she's written it with a feather pen, and the lime-green ink she used isn't helping.

"It's gotta be buckskin, because that's what he wore," I say. "A raccoon skin cap and buckskins."

"That makes more sense."

I type the last few lines before realizing we don't have the paper Mr. Ramirez gave us for formatting. He'll take off ten points minimum if the margins are off or I put the title in the wrong spot. That's a B before he even starts reading it. I don't tell Hamilton, because he's stressed out enough, and instead use my best judgment to make the changes. I push PRINT on two copies and race toward the printer.

"I don't think I can handle this," Hamilton says when we finally scarf down our lunches. "Too much stress."

"If you can't handle this, then you definitely can't handle working with me. This is just grades. I'm talking about people's lives."

"It's my first day," Hamilton argues as he takes a bite of his chicken patty on a bun. "I bet you weren't perfect on your first day."

"Yes, I was. I had to be."

Hamilton sticks out his tongue, which is covered with chewed-up bun.

"Gross."

He takes another bite and smiles, this time bits of broccoli in his teeth. "Give me a second chance," he says as food sprays onto his tray. I laugh out loud and am reprimanded with a stern "shhhh" from the librarian. I look at the clock; we are down to a minute.

"Okay," I say, getting ready to speed through my plan. "Use a restroom pass during band to get out of class, and I'll meet you in the courtyard. He always skips fifth period, so we'll be able to find him back behind the portable classrooms. He hangs out there when he skips."

"Who skips?"

"Santos," I say as quickly as possible, hoping Hamilton won't make a fuss.

"Santos?" he says with his mouth full of chicken patty. "I *knew* he was your boyfriend!"

"Enough with the boyfriend thing! I'll tell you when someone is actually my boyfriend. Santos was held back in fifth grade, so his voice has matured already and he sounds like an adult. I technically don't have a meeting with him until next week, but I already found some information on his foster mom. I'll share that and then ask him. I can give him the next session for free in exchange for the call."

The bell rings, and we both swig down the last of our chocolate milks.

"Don't dump those in here!" the librarian chides. "Take them to the garbage in the cafeteria."

We scoop up our backpacks, balancing our trays with one hand.

"You think he'll help?" Hamilton asks as we push open the library doors.

"I think so. He's a foster kid. He knows what a bad family is like." The stream of students begins to separate us. "Don't be late!"

Hamilton nods before disappearing into the mass of moving kids.

# RECRUITMENT

Across the field, Santos is standing next to the shed where they keep all the gym supplies, like dumbbells and jump ropes. He's peeling off the tape from the motivational posters adhered to the side, sending them fluttering to the ground, one by one. Down goes a crew and their rowboat, their cry of TEAMWORK sinking with them. Then a mountain climber with AMBITION joins the dirt. Finally, some lone person in the Sahara desert falls to the ground, unable to handle the all-caps CHALLENGE.

"That's him?" Hamilton whispers as we cross the track. "Why is he out here?"

"Shush," I say as we near Santos. "Stand back a bit.

Let me talk to him first, and then I'll call you over if I need you."

"Sure, sure. I can be cool."

I doubt that, but I hustle toward Santos.

"You can't do that if you want to stay at your new home," I say when I'm close, bending to pick up one of the fallen posters. He doesn't turn around right away, so I shout his name. When he does finally turn, I notice the earbuds in his ears and the glare on his face. He better not expect to take his bad mood out on me.

"You said next week."

"You don't look busy now. And I've already found a few things on your foster mom." I unzip my backpack and grab the manila envelope full of the documents I compiled yesterday during lunch. He frowns.

"Seriously, if you don't want the information, just tell me. Oh, and take out your headphones. You can at least be polite when I did all this for you."

"You didn't do this for me," he says as he presses his earbuds in tighter, heavy beats escaping into the air. "You don't even know me."

I sigh. "Maybe I don't, but I do know some stuff about Alma Graves, and that's why you hired me."

He doesn't respond, just kicks one of the posters with his foot. "Who's the kid?"

I turn to see Hamilton suddenly looking off into the sky, dragging his foot in a semicircle in the dust. This must be his I'm-minding-my-own-business pose.

"My foster brother."

At his mention, Hamilton steps one foot forward, bending into a small bow. "Hamilton Jennings."

Weirdo. I can't take him anywhere.

"What's he doing here?"

"Ignore him." I give Hamilton the stink eye, and he backpedals like he's moving away from a grizzly bear. I turn back to Santos. "So, Alma Graves…" I point to her picture on the first page. I talk him through the highlights: her job, her house, the motivational posts on her Facebook, which match the posters he's sent tossing to the ground. I show him the resumé I found on the county clerk's office home page, and even a picture of her from her high school yearbook. He's silent as I go through the pages, but he occasionally runs a finger along a sentence, so I know he's listening.

"She used to do emergency nights, so it's possible someone has spent a night or two there and can tell us more about her house. I'll keep asking. I used the address on her resumé to pull up some old real estate listing pictures, and the house looks nice: two bedrooms, so you should have your own, a little backyard."

I hand Santos the packet and ask him when he moves in.

"Tuesday."

"She's out of this zone, so you'll probably have to go to a new school. Unless she gets you a waiver. Then you can probably stay until the end of the semester. At least until the end of the grading period."

"I know."

"New schools are an add-on to your regular package if you want it. I can help with collecting materials from teachers, grades, shot records. I even once helped a kid skip a grade."

"Could you get me outta basic math? I used to be advanced."

I swallow my shock. "Probably. We can talk about it once you've moved." I take out my calendar and a pen. Suddenly there's a yelp behind us, and we both turn to see Hamilton on the ground.

"Sorry, sorry," he says. I have no idea how that happened. I take a deep breath.

"If your foster mom lets you stay at our school, we'll do your session in person, otherwise we can do it online...." I flip through the pages of my full-color calendar. Man, it turned out great. "Next Friday? You'll have been there a few days. Be sure to fill out the First

Week Information Packet in your envelope as soon as you get there. You need to do it while your first impressions are fresh. It helps me do more detailed research for you." I also add it to my family files in case anyone gets sent there again. "That is about all I got. Questions?"

He shakes his head.

"You should try to talk a little when you first get there. You're setting yourself up for trouble if you don't."

He shrugs. It's his life, I guess. "How much I owe you?"

"About that," I say as he slides off one strap of his backpack, turning it around to the front of his body so he can unzip it. He takes out a white plastic bag from Walgreens and hands it to me. Inside are two boxes of Ticonderoga pencils (the number one pencil), a set of colored Sharpies, and a three-pack of glue sticks (generic brand—I'll have to remind him about my brand-name-only policy), and a family size bag of Hot Cheetos. "I want you to make a phone call for me. If you do, I'll cancel your charges, and you can return these or use them for any follow-up sessions, like the New School one I mentioned."

Santos looks out across the field toward the people spending their afternoon on Congress Avenue. If he was going to say no, he would have walked away.

"What kinda call?"

"To CPS."

I hear Hamilton whisper "Child Protective Services" behind me. He's been trying to learn all the foster acronyms. He even made flash cards.

"His mom's crazy?" Santos asks, and Hamilton's head shoots up.

"Hey! My mom's not crazy!"

Santos scowls, and I raise a hand to shush Hamilton.

"It's not for his mom. It's for a Crossroads kid."

Santos shrugs his shoulders. "Tell a teacher. They're always calling CPS."

"It's best if adults don't get involved. I don't have a lot of time to save this kid from the worst home of her life. If you don't want to do it, fine. Just give me the bag."

I snatch it out of his hand and start marching across the field.

"That's it?" Hamilton whispers as he joins me. "You didn't even push him!"

I ignore him, knowing I need to keep quiet for the question coming in three, two, one....

"What do you want me to say?"

I turn around. "I'll have a script. Basically, that you have suspicions that this family is using drugs."

"Are they?"

"No," I say, taking a step toward him. "The truth is worse, but apparently no one is interested in investigating the real reason."

"When?"

His scowl softens, and for a moment I see it: the smallest adjustment in a face frozen by years of frowning. Hope.

"As soon as possible. Monday, if we can. We need to find an unlocked classroom during fourth or fifth period. All the principals will be in the cafeteria for A and B lunches. The hallways should be clear."

"We can use Mr. Ramirez's room," Hamilton says from behind me. Santos and I turn to him. "He always goes and gets a coffee from 7-Eleven during A lunch, and the lock on his door doesn't work."

I ask Santos if he can get out of fourth period, and he nods. "I got A lunch."

"Fourth period, then. Right after attendance. We'll get a pass to visit his room, just in case he hasn't left when we get there. Here."

I hand Santos back the bag of supplies and he clutches it in one hand, adjusting his earbuds with the other.

"See you Monday. Don't forget to fill out your First Week Information Packet. And keep practicing your Front Door Face."

He continues to push the gravel with the scuffed toe of his old tennis shoes. If he were a different kind of client, I might give him a side hug. Say I know how it feels. The days before you meet your new family are always the worst because your imagination is deadly. Even if they end up being awful, at least you'll know when you meet them. Then you can deal. When all you have is a name and a date, you have nothing to do but worry. I could say all that. Instead I say, "Good luck."

"I don't need it." His face is hard as he slides his backpack around to his back. I hope he doesn't need luck, either.

"Let's go," I tell Hamilton, and we race across the track toward the main building.

"That guy should not be your boyfriend," he says when we make it to the front gate. "He is not pleasant."

I laugh out loud as we head to our separate classes.

# SANTOS MAKES THE CALL

Alone in Mr. Ramirez's room, I wait by the door, my hand on the handle and my cheek pressed to the wood. The door is cracked the smallest bit, and I resist the urge to poke my head out and look again. I check the clock above me. It's a few minutes past noon, fifteen minutes into fourth period. Hamilton and Santos should be here by now. It's possible Santos bailed, but I thought I could at least count on Hamilton to show up.

Suddenly, the door handle turns, and I yelp, realizing I have nowhere to hide. Thankfully, Santos's face appears in the open door. He's smiling, which is a first.

"Whoa. Chill." He slides past me and closes the door behind him.

"You're late."

"So's the little dude."

"I'll worry about him. You worry about you."

I pull the script out of my back pocket. It's wrinkled now, but I didn't want to bring my full portfolio. Now that I think about it, I would have looked less suspicious if caught. I could say I was dropping off an assignment or something.

"So, we gonna do this?" Santos asks as he scans the room for the phone. "I have places to be."

"You don't even go to class."

"Doesn't mean I don't have places to be."

I shake my head. "The phone is by the back window." With Santos here, we could start, but I feel a strange desire to wait for Hamilton. "We'll wait one more minute, and if he doesn't show, we'll call."

"You're the boss."

Santos hops on top of a desk, his feet swinging back and forth like he's at the playground. He pops his gum a few times while he studies something on the ceiling. I decide to risk one last look and creak the door open so I can see out with one eye. A couple of kids pass, and then there's a long stretch of no one. Then I spot him, scuttling down the hall, bent at the waist like he's ducking under invisible branches.

"Hamilton! Stand up!" I whisper, and he jumps. He sighs when he sees me. "Get in here!"

"I'm sorry I'm late. I was trying to get out of there, but then we had this problem about analogies, and Piper kept saying that 'eye' cannot go with potato even though Ms. Cooper told us that an eye can be part of a potato because it's some old-timey word, but anyway, Piper got me into it, and then I had to look it up in the dictionary for her...."

"Enough," I say, pushing him toward the phone. "We don't have time."

"Should I be a lookout?"

"No. By the time you see him in the hallway, there's no escape. You're just here to..." I don't really know why he is here. I make up a job. "Take notes."

"Yes!" Hamilton says with a fist pump before pulling out his miniature reporter's notebook and the golf pencil. He begins scribbling, announcing each word. "October fifteenth, 12:05 PM. Mr. Ramirez's room."

I don't listen to the rest of his notes and instead turn to prep Santos. He's looking at Hamilton with a raised eyebrow.

"Here's the number. Your name is Victor Gonzalez. You don't know the child, but you know the family—"

"Is that 'Gonzalez' with a z or with an s?" Hamilton asks.

"What?"

Hamilton repeats the question.

"It doesn't matter. It's a fake name," I explain.

"Sorry. Just want to make sure the notes are accurate." He takes another spin in the rolling chair before continuing to narrate his notes. "Student will be calling as a Mr. Victor Gonzalez; that's 'Gonzalez' with a $z$."

I take a deep breath and turn back to Santos. "The family are your neighbors. Here's their address. I used Google Maps to find a house nearby, just in case they ask where you live."

I point to the highlighted address.

"I got this," Santos says, and I hope he's right.

I dial the number before putting the phone on speaker. I take a step back so Santos can move closer. We stand side by side as it rings. I hold the script, ready to point to his lines in case he gets lost. Hamilton sits directly behind us, continuing to slowly spin in circles as he scribbles. Santos's face is calm while the phone rings, but he bites his lip when the line clicks.

"Texas Department of Family and Protective Services Abuse Hotline. Are you calling to report the abuse of a child or of an adult over the age of sixty-five?" The female voice sounds bored.

"A child," Santos says without missing a beat.

"And your name, sir." A crunch.

"Victor Gonzalez."

"Is that 'Gonzalez' with a *z* or with an *s*?" the voice asks, and Hamilton lets out a triumphant "I told you so!"

Santos and I both turn and glare, and he shrinks back into the chair, sliding a few inches away from us. In a whisper, Hamilton adds, "I was RIGHT!"

"Excuse me?" the voice asks, and Santos confirms that it is "Gonzalez" with a *z*.

"And your relationship to the victim?" More crunching. Is she eating lunch?

"I don't know the kid. I'm calling about a foster family. My neighbors. They were talking about getting a foster kid, and I suspect they've been doing drugs in their backyard."

"Do you have proof of illegal substance use?" A swallow.

"I didn't see it, but I could smell it."

Suddenly there is a loud crash, and we both turn to see Hamilton wide-eyed, the rolling chair having collided into a stack of Mr. Ramirez's bins. The floor is now covered with highlighters and glue sticks.

"I'm sorry," Hamilton mouths, and my finger flies to my lips.

"Is everything okay, Mr. Gonzalez?"

Santos looks furious as he explains that everything is fine, he's just at work.

"What's the contact information for the foster family in question?" the voice continues.

He reads the Nickersons' names and address. "It's about a kid," Santos continues. "So you should probably check it out."

"We will do the best we can. Is this the best number to contact you at if we have further questions?"

"This is my work phone. You should call me on my cell."

He makes up a number. He sounds so formal, too, like all these words were just buried inside him, waiting to burst out. I can suddenly picture him in a suit with a briefcase.

"Do you have any other information to report?"

"Nope."

With one final crunch and a thank-you, the voice hangs up, and the three of us are left staring at the phone.

"Can I cheer now?" asks Hamilton, back in the chair after picking up the supplies.

I smile. "A small one."

Hamilton whoops and spins three times. Then we

hear it. The turning of the door handle. I shove Hamilton out of the chair and under Mr. Ramirez's desk. He doesn't see us right away as he turns on the classroom lights, balancing a tray of coffee cups in his hand and holding a croissant in his mouth. When he turns to us, he yelps, the croissant falling onto the cups below him.

"Pavi! What are you doing in here?" He brushes crumbs off his lime-green tie. Quickly, I grab Santos's hand. Better he thinks we are here on a date than a robbery. Mr. Ramirez frowns when he recognizes Santos.

"None of your business," Santos says, not letting go of my hand. I was not planning to make trouble, but Santos seems determined. I can feel Hamilton shifting under the desk, and I give him a nudge with my foot to remind him to stay quiet.

"Excuse me?" Mr. Ramirez says, setting the coffees down on a desk and making his way toward us. "You're in my classroom. In the dark. Without permission." He looks over at me. "I'm disappointed in your choices, especially yours, Pavi."

Mr. Ramirez seems to believe our fake reason for being here. I drop Santos's hand, feeling guilty that one of my favorite teachers is disappointed in me. I wish I could explain, say it was all for a good reason. That I'm really a Robin Hood, not a villain. Maybe saving Meridee will turn me into a bit of a bad guy.

"You two need to come with me to the office."

With one last glance at Hamilton, I follow Mr. Ramirez out the door, Santos trailing us. As we walk to the main office, I imagine Hamilton crawling out from under the desk, dusting off his knees, and slipping out into the hallway. Back to class. Back to being a star student, untainted by me.

# THE POWER OF BEFORE

Santos and I sit outside the assistant principals' offices. He stretches all the way down to his tennis shoes before swinging his arms above his head, grazing the framed photo above us. "I gotta get out of here," he mutters. I'm sure he's waited for the principal hundreds of times. I've been in a principal's office before. Once to get an award, but mostly to talk about my foster families.

I close my eyes, leaning my head back against the wall, Santos's bouncing foot now causing mine to vibrate. I need to think of a story, should maybe get Santos on board with a lie.

"Oh my god, Pavi? Is that you?"

I cringe, not ready to open my eyes to the smug face I know I'll see.

"Hi, Piper."

I open my eyes to see Piper across the counter from me, her OFFICE AIDE badge twirling around her finger as she stares at the two of us.

"What are you doing in here?" she whispers, as if the secretaries don't already know why I'm here. Or even care. "Are you...with him?"

"I'm waiting for Ms. Taylor. Cougar Pride Award."

Piper absorbs the lie, her face saying she doesn't quite believe me. She grabs a stack of papers out of a small wooden bin. "I'm glad to hear you're doing so well... if only our Davy Crockett lyrics could have turned out like that. Mr. Ramirez already put the grades online. Eighty. Two."

Ugh. Worse than I thought, but I don't have time to deal with that right now. It was a major project grade, but we can still bounce back from that.

Piper stares at me before quickly turning on her heel, almost bumping into Ms. Taylor, the seventh-grade principal, who's coming in the front door. Ms. Taylor listens to her walkie-talkie as she makes her way around the front counter. As usual, she's dressed like she's running for president, in a red business skirt and suit jacket and very shiny blonde hair. She only needs a tiny American flag pin. She stops a few inches from my chair. "Pavi Sharma. Didn't expect this call."

I stay silent, pleading the fifth like we learned in Intro to Law.

"Ms. Jennings is on the way over. She had to get someone to cover her class."

Noooooo. I knew they'd call Marjorie, but I didn't think they would make her come here!

"Santos, since you're in eighth grade, Ms. Williams will take care of you. Do you know if anyone's called your parents?"

I cringe, but Santos doesn't flinch.

"No."

"We'll look up their number and give them a call, then."

"Good luck with that."

Ms. Taylor's eyebrows fly up her forehead. "Excuse me? Don't take that attitude with me."

"I don't got attitude, Miss."

I wait for him to explain that he's in foster care, but he just leans back in his chair, fiddling with the cord on his black hoodie.

"Williams, pick up," Ms. Taylor barks into her walkie-talkie. "Have you called Santos's parents yet? About the incident in Mr. Ramirez's room?"

Ms. Williams's voice crackles over the radio. "He's in foster. His new placement came up to school Monday, so we have her info, but he isn't legally in her custody for a few days. Check his file to see what number to call."

"Ten-four," Ms. Taylor says before looking at Santos with a familiar wash of guilt. It's the same look teachers give me when they ask if I want to call my mom or my dad. Or when they give an assignment to interview a grandparent. Marjorie always loans me her mom for my interviews, but when I bring in the required pictures, they know we don't go together. When I did my heritage report on Ireland, where Marjorie's family is from, people kept asking, "But where are you *really* from?" They knew my dark hair and dark eyes didn't match the redheaded, freckled faces looking out from the photo. I know I'm Indian American, but I don't know exactly where in India my ancestors are from. I don't have any stories to tell about holidays or foods or geography. Ma was born in Houston. I never met my grandparents. Or my dad. It was easier to choose Ireland. And Marjorie had a lot of stuff with shamrocks on it.

"Santos, you can wait here for Ms. Williams. Pavi, we can head into my office."

As I stand up, Hamilton peeks through the front office windows, his head just above the counter.

"Are you okay?" he mouths, and I shake my head, hoping he'll read it as "Not now. Go away," and not "I'm doing terrible! Come in here and save me!"

Ms. Taylor heads into her office, and I quickly mouth "Go" at Hamilton before turning to follow her. Ms. Taylor is already furiously typing something on her computer, her manicured nails clicking against the keys. Every few seconds, her radio beeps with messages about student names and locations. She answers a few, practically ignoring me, until we both hear Marjorie's voice.

"I'm Marjorie Jennings, Pavi Sharma's guardian. I'm here to see Ms. Taylor."

My heart beats frantically in my chest as I wait for her to enter the room. I've never been in trouble before. I am a good foster kid. It wouldn't be smart business if I didn't follow my own rules.

"Sorry it took me a while to get here," Marjorie says, taking her seat.

"Not a problem at all." Ms. Taylor rolls her chair closer to her desk and the two of us.

Marjorie finally looks at me, her eyes a mix of

disappointment and, thankfully, worry. "What happened, Pav?"

Before I open my mouth, Ms. Taylor has answered for me. "She was found in a classroom with an eighth-grade boy. And the lights were off."

With the word "off," she gives Marjorie a knowing look.

"What were you doing in there?" Marjorie asks.

"We were just talking," I say, and Ms. Taylor rolls her eyes, pushing a strand of platinum-blonde hair behind her ear.

"Really?" Ms. Taylor asks. "With the lights off?"

"Yes," I say, looking her firmly in the eyes. "Just talking."

"Is he your boyfriend?" Marjorie asks, her tone gentle but probing.

"No. We used to be at the same shelter."

Marjorie's shoulders relax and even Ms. Taylor gives me the face. And then I realize I have my out.

"Lenny, our old coordinator at the shelter…he's… retiring…so I wanted Santos to take a card to him, since he was going to be there one last night before he moves. To his new home. He's really worried about it. It's his first placement."

Ms. Taylor clicks her tongue and shakes her head. Marjorie doesn't seem to completely buy it.

"And the only time you could give him this card was during class? In a dark classroom?"

"It was stupid," I say, now looking at Marjorie. "But we're not supposed to be in the hall, and we didn't have the lights on because we were just in there a few seconds before Mr. Ramirez came."

Marjorie reaches for my hand. "You need to be more careful, Pavi. People are going to make a lot of assumptions now that you're older, especially if you're spending time with an older boy."

"I just wanted to make sure Lenny got his card. He…he did a lot for me."

"I know, Pav," Marjorie says, squeezing my hand. "I could have taken it for you. Or let you go after school. Just talk to me, okay?"

"Or me," Ms. Taylor says, reaching across the desk to squeeze my other hand. I'm about to be pulled in half. Sensing the weirdness, Marjorie lets go.

"What will her consequence be?" Marjorie asks, and Ms. Taylor smiles.

"It's her first time, so we'll let it go. Just make sure you stay out of restricted places."

"Of course." This is turning out better than I could have imagined. I hope it's going as well for Santos.

"I have to get back to school," Marjorie says, standing up and pushing her chair toward the desk. "I'll see you and Hambone later." She gives me a hug before walking out of the office. I go to follow her, when Ms. Taylor stops me.

"Pavi." She sighs, pulling me into a side hug. "You can always come here to talk. I am here. For. You."

I give her my best Front Door Face and escape out of her office.

# HAMILTON'S BIG ADVENTURE

After school, I wait for Hamilton on the brick ledge outside the main building. He's ten minutes late, so only a few students are still hanging out by the flagpole, waiting for their parents. I should be working on the mountain of homework Hamilton and I were assigned, since we already got a late grade in math and an 82 on Mr. Ramirez's Texas history project. I should be trying to get caught up, maybe even get ahead, but instead, I bite the end of a piece of hair while I replay the phone call over and over again. Will they actually go investigate? Will there be anything to see? Just as I move to create split ends in another strand of hair, Hamilton comes bursting out of the door, dragging his baritone behind him, the plastic of its case scratching along the sidewalk.

"Oh. My. Gosh. Pavi! That was the most exhilarating day of my life! I've never been in that kind of danger!" He drops the enormous black case to the ground and bends at his waist, taking a deep breath. "Well, one time I was trapped on the top of the Ferris wheel for fifteen minutes while they fixed a mechanical issue, but that was nothing compared to today."

"Today wasn't real danger, either," I say, swinging my legs over the edge to face him. "You didn't even get caught."

"But I could have been!" He hops up to sit beside me, missing the first hop, but then managing to get a seat. "I was watching Mr. Ramirez's feet as he was talking to you and thinking, *This is it. Your life as an A-plus, no-detention student is over. You're now officially a bad kid.* But then he stopped and you two walked out, and I was so relieved!" He stops. "But I would have done it for you. Gotten caught. If I needed to."

I roll my eyes. "Thanks."

"Did you get in trouble? Santos has lunch detention for the rest of the week!"

"What?" I say, leaning closer to Hamilton so the stragglers outside don't hear our business. "He has detention? How do you know that?"

"I went and found him after school. That's why I'm late." Hamilton reaches down to grab a water bottle from his backpack. He takes a big swig before offering it to me. I decline. I don't want his backwash. I want details.

"And he told you he has detention?"

"Yep. The whole week, because he wouldn't say anything when Ms. Williams questioned him. Can you believe it? Not one word. And Ms. Williams is super scary! She's made, like, half the eighth graders cry. If it was me, I would have cracked. Totally." Hamilton hoots before taking another swig of his water. "Honestly, I thought Santos was a bit creepy at first, with all the skulking, but man, is he impressive! His adult voice during the phone call…he sounded like a real man! I bet he's going to have a beard by freshman year."

He was pretty impressive. I hop off the ledge, realizing if I wait for Hamilton to finish talking we will be here until tomorrow morning. I pick up the front of his baritone case, and he grabs the other end.

"And then to just walk into the principal's office, plop his feet up on the desk…"

"He did not put his feet up on the desk," I say as I step over a crack in the sidewalk.

"Well, not literally, but figuratively, he totally did. He's like a rock! Like a silent…rock!"

"Maybe he should be *your* boyfriend."

Hamilton shrugs. "Not my type, but if he was, totally. That is a cool dude. Minus the not-going-to-class and constant glaring."

"I'm glad you know what you want."

At the stoplight, we mix with the people waiting in line at the new taco restaurant. A giant man in workout clothes towers over Hamilton. We rest the case on the sidewalk as we wait for the light to change. Our afternoon routine.

"Was Mom mad?" Hamilton asks as the light turns and we begin moving across the street.

"Not really. Worried, mostly, but I told them a story about the shelter, so I didn't get in trouble. We probably should be careful, though, not to make her suspicious. Let's get our homework done right away tonight. Our math assignment was late and...we got an eighty-two on the lyrics assignment."

Hamilton gasps. "No! How did that happen? We turned that in on time."

"I don't know yet, but we can't afford another low grade or your mom will start to think something's up."

"Maybe she'll just think we are going through a defiant stage of adolescence."

"I don't think that helps us."

"So, do we just wait now? To find out if they're going to do something about the bad family?"

"For a few days, at least. I need to get back to Crossroads and see when she's supposed to move in with them. I'll try to find out if Lenny has heard anything. He should know right away if something is up."

"Cool," Hamilton says as he sidesteps a puddle from last night's rainstorm. "I'm going to type up the notes for us. I have a folder labeled COMPUTER GAMES so Mom won't find it, even if she's looking."

"Smart. 'Pavi's Secret Mission Notes' was too obvious?"

He laughs. "Pavi *and* Hamilton's Secret Mission Notes."

I smile. That's right. It's our secret mission now, and step one is complete.

~

When Marjorie gets home, Hamilton and I are already through our math homework and the last of the ice-cream sandwiches. We should have more done than we do, but Hamilton kept pulling out his little notebook and reliving this afternoon. He's even made some corrections (of what, I have no idea. I didn't ask. Didn't want to encourage).

"Hi, Pav. Hi, Hambone." Marjorie drops her purse on the counter and picks up the empty ice-cream bar box, frowning at the four wrappers stuffed inside. "I see you got a lot of eating done. Did you get much homework done?"

Simultaneously we hold up our math packets and beam identical smiles at her.

"Anything else left to do?" Marjorie asks, flipping the switch on the coffeepot we already filled with fresh grounds. There was no Crock-Pot to start today.

"We both have English, and I have Spanish homework," Hamilton says.

"I have one article review for science," I add.

Her side to us, Marjorie takes a deep inhale of the brewing coffee. "Any work for Mr. Ramirez? You know I expect all assignments to be your very best work...."

Hamilton's wide eyes flick to me, and he mouths "She knows."

Of course she knows. She checks our grades online. You can't fool a mom who is also a teacher.

"No, ma'am," I say, and Marjorie turns to us.

"Hambone, why don't you go practice your baritone for a bit before dinner? I was thinking pizza tonight?"

"I already practiced my twenty minutes," Hamilton

says in a bit of a huff. He always practices right when we get home. It's her rule.

"Go ahead and do an extra fifteen, then. You know you wanted extra credit in that class anyway."

"I don't need extra credit. I have an A. You can't get higher than that."

"Do it for the love of the music, then."

Hamilton gives his mom a suspicious look before slinking off the counter stool. I don't want him to leave. I don't want to be alone with Marjorie until I've figured out what to say. When Hamilton gets to the doorway to the kitchen, he stops and turns. "Ten minutes."

Marjorie smiles, filling her cup with coffee. "That's fine."

My stomach turns as I pretend to show my work for a math problem, trying hard to not make eye contact while Marjorie adds cream and sugar to her mug. She takes a sip before bustling around the kitchen, tossing out the ice-cream bar box and unpacking her lunch bag. It's the calm before the storm. Or the rain shower. Or light gust of wind. She was so calm in the office, but maybe she was waiting until we got home in private to get mad at me. She's never yelled at me before. Maybe she will today. Or maybe I'll just get the Voice. And the Look.

"So, Pavi…"

I look up from my math homework like I have no idea where this conversation could be headed. Would you like to know what new book I'm reading? Or whether I've laid out my clothes for tomorrow? I have great answers to those questions!

"Yes?" I ask, my pencil still in my hand so she knows I'm ready to jump back into this very challenging homework at any second. The sound of Hamilton playing his warm-up march comes through the air vents. He's playing louder than necessary and pounding his foot to the tempo.

"You didn't seem comfortable speaking in front of your principal, so I wanted to check in about what happened at school."

I drop my eyes before looking back at her, that pencil staying right where it is. I don't know what I was expecting, but it wasn't that. It would almost be easier if she yelled. I know how to handle yelling.

"It's okay to have private things you don't want to share with me. I get that."

Marjorie knows about keeping the past quiet. She told me when I first moved in about Hamilton's dad: how he left when Hamilton was just born and how she moved down here to live closer to her parents. They never talk about him; it's like one day Hamilton popped into her life, and as far as we know, she's never dated anybody else.

"Is there anything else you want to tell me about what happened today?" The way she's looking at me makes me consider saying yes. Maybe even telling her about Meridee, telling her everything. But I don't.

"I told you everything at school."

Marjorie sets her coffee cup on the counter. "Then I'm glad it was no big deal. I do want you to know that you're getting to the age that..."

Oh my gosh, please let this not be a changing-body talk. I don't need a foster mother–foster daughter heart-to-heart. They already told us all this in fifth grade, but foster parents always want to have the special growing-up moments: learning to ride a bike, first-day-of-school photos.

Marjorie continues talking about feelings and my changing body (yep...it's that kinda talk) and my hand is starting to cramp from holding this pencil in the air, but I refuse to set it down.

"Just know you can trust me, Pav. With the things you don't think I'll get. I don't want you to keep secrets because you're worried I'll be mad or unhappy with you."

She reaches across the counter, and I drop the pencil so I can squeeze her extended palm.

"You can go stop the music," Marjorie says, giving my hand one final squeeze. I hop off my stool.

"I should have bought him a harp," she mutters as I head for the stairs.

## OCTOBER BIRTHDAYS

The next day, I stand outside the main office window after school, staring at a bouquet of roses with a huge heart balloon floating above them. When I was younger, I always wanted someone to send me a large HAPPY BIRTHDAY balloon with a couple of small colored ones beside it and maybe a teddy bear. I knew Ma couldn't afford any of that, but I envied the kids who would get the small yellow slip from the office, asking them to come down to pick up their gift. We all knew to look through the office's glass window when we walked to gym or music. Those balloons would be waiting on the counter, a floating symbol of the kind of love that everyone is promised but not everyone gets.

Ma did give me her own gifts sometimes, stories as she cooked or a song as I got ready for school. Those were my roses, but just like real flowers, they didn't last.

I want Meridee to have a chance for balloons. I have to go to Crossroads and see her. I don't know if Child Protective Services would have already made the call, but I can ask Lenny. At the very least, I can figure out when Meridee's moving in with them. I can start the countdown.

~

They're setting up decorations for the October birthday parties when I get to Crossroads. Lenny and Keisha are standing on chairs, trying to hang the same HAPPY BIRTHDAY banner they used when I was there. The cardboard letters are scuffed along the edges and part of the letter *R* is ripped off where a piece of tape was stuck to it. They're playing music out of someone's phone, and kids come in and out of the room, helping with a job before they get bored and leave for something else. I wave at the two boys, Jackson and Simon, who are sitting in the corner attempting to blow up balloons.

Without a helium tank, they won't float above the table, but they're fun to kick around on the floor, especially for the little kids.

"Hey, Ms. Sharma," Lenny shouts as he spots me. "Come over and hold this end."

Keisha smiles at me as I move over to Lenny's edge of the banner. He hands me the frayed edge of the string. "Hold this here a second. I'm gonna tape this up."

"How've you been, Pav?" Keisha asks, and I tell her about school as I hold up my end of the string. "Hey! Get down!" Keisha yells, and I turn my head to see Jackson and Simon standing on the back of the couch, ready to dive into the small pile of balloons on the worn carpet.

"Cannonball," Jackson yells, but Keisha stops them with a forceful "Boys!" Unfortunately, her command doesn't get ahead of Simon's momentum and he tumbles headfirst down the couch and onto the floor.

"Dude, let's video that!" Jackson cheers as he pulls Simon back up. "Keisha, can we use your phone?"

"No, and down off the couch now." She turns back to the decorations.

"Is Meridee here?" I ask as Lenny hands me the old tape dispenser.

"She should be in the playroom. We haven't enrolled her in after-school programs yet," Keisha says as she climbs down from her chair.

"She still has a placement?"

Lenny rubs his chin before answering. "Yep. Her caseworker called this afternoon and said things are on track. They want to set up a family visit first, but then she'll move in on Thursday."

My stomach drops. "So, everything's okay with the family?"

Lenny frowns. "You're still thinking about that? I told you it's all good."

"Have you been there? To at least check it out?"

"What's all this about?" Keisha asks as she tears off a couple of pieces of tape.

"Nothing," Lenny answers before I can explain myself. "Pavi's worried about an old foster family of hers, but everything is fine. I checked in with Meridee's caseworker, and she said there's nothing to worry about. Pavi needs to focus on school. All those volcanoes."

He winks at me, but his smile is infuriating right now. I don't know why I bothered asking him for help. Apparently, it's up to me. Again.

"You've got enough to worry about, Pav," Keisha

adds, reaching out to squeeze my arm. "Let us do our jobs for a while."

I fight the urge to scream. "I'm going to go see Meridee now."

Their good-byes are muffled by the party supplies they are holding in their mouths. I pick up my backpack from the place I dropped it. Beside it is a hand-made card on a folded piece of printer paper. "Happy Birthday" is scrawled across the front in loopy crayon. There's a child on the front. No balloons, no friends, no sun in the corner of the page. I set the card up on the table.

I have a few days to make a new plan. I hope it's enough time.

I find Meridee in the playroom, her body the eye in the center of a Lego-Barbie hurricane. I crouch down on the ground beside her, moving aside the scattered Lego blocks and Barbie legs.

"Hi, Meridee. Do you remember me? Pavi?"

She looks up from the Barbie doll head she has been brushing. It doesn't have a body, and she has one finger poked in the base of its neck, creating a stand for her beauty parlor.

She smiles but doesn't say anything.

"I like your Barbie."

I look around the floor to find a matching body, but realize that all the other Barbie bodies are white and Meridee has found the only black head. Who knows where the body is.

"Her name is Mama, and she's going to the mall," Meridee says, stroking the fake black locks with a miniature yellow comb.

"The mall sounds fun. Is she going shopping?"

Meridee shakes her head. "She's getting a pretzel with nacho cheese."

"That sounds yummy."

While she brushes, I search the ground for matching body parts so I can put together the Barbies. I find a leg that matches a top with both arms and try to fasten it back in its socket. Meridee and I sit in silence, both concentrating on our projects. I finally manage to put one together, though it's missing an arm. I hand Meridee the doll.

"Here's a friend for Mama. She also likes pretzels with nacho cheese."

"Mama doesn't need a friend. She has me."

"She has you," I repeat, not sure what else to say.

Suddenly, Meridee drops the head she had so carefully groomed. "Are you gonna take me to Frankie's?"

"I don't know Frankie."

"Frankie has two dogs. Hot Dog and Griz."

I smile, picking up the doll head and handing it back to Meridee.

"Mama likes Frankie. He lets us park our car there, and when I have to potty, he lets me come inside."

I pull out an astronaut jumpsuit and carefully shove the bent Barbie feet into the skinny silver pants.

"Sometimes I let Hot Dog in the car with me. Mama yells 'cause he gets hair all on everything, but he's so cute and drooly. I call him Drooly Hot Dog."

I search the bin and pull out a piece of rainbow-colored yarn that someone must have used for a scarf and twist it around the Barbie's neck.

"I wanna go to Frankie's," she says, her brown eyes staring into mine.

"I think you're gonna stay here for a while, okay?"

She wrinkles up her nose and I'm afraid she's preparing to wail. Instead, she sneezes.

"I wanna go to Frankie's," she repeats. Over and over. She picks up the comb and grabs the newly dressed Barbie from my hand. I don't know who Frankie is, but I remember wanting to go back. I remember hating the newness of my life, from the sheets to the strange meals to the other kids. I wanted to go back for a long time, too.

Maybe she will.

Maybe she won't.

But if she doesn't, even if she never goes back to Frankie's, eventually she'll be happy again. She'll learn to like her new family.

That is, unless she ends up at the Nickersons'.

## SOLVED

I t's 8:00 PM and Hamilton still isn't back from Piper's. For hours, I've been listening to Marjorie hum along to the radio while she and I scrapbook. I apply a ruler sticker to the corner of last year's report card and feel every single second while I sit here waiting. Finally, we hear a knock on the door.

"Hambone," Marjorie says, shaking her head. "He probably forgot his key. Can you let him in?"

I'm already out of my chair and headed toward the door. There's another knock before I pull the handle.

"I'm com...Oh. My. God. What happened to you?"

Hamilton's eyes glare at me through their black-lined rims.

"Don't ask any questions," he says, and I couldn't ask anything if I wanted to because I'm speechless. He takes a step inside the house and sets his backpack on the floor. Under the hallway lights, I can finally take in the full picture: Hamilton the gothic centaur, a creature with a band-geek body and the head of a moody vampire. His hair is slicked down to the side, covering his left eye, and there appears to be a smattering of black glitter gleaming in the strands. In addition to the eyeliner, he has uneven black lips and his face looks paler than usual. It's then that I notice the flecks of white dusting his shoulders.

"What's that white...?"

"Flour," he answers, his shoulders hunched in misery. "Can we talk about something else?"

Just then we hear the radio click off, and Marjorie shuffles into the hallway. Hamilton turns toward the door, but there's no way he's hiding this.

"Hey, Hambo...oh!" Marjorie stops, apparently speechless at the sight, too. She takes a step toward him, smiling before breaking into her giant laughter, her whole body shaking as she grabs the stair railing to keep her balance. I can't help laughing, too, and even Hamilton grins, the black lipstick staining the creases at the corners of his lips.

"Okay, okay, sorry, sweetie," Marjorie says, finally calming herself. "That was rude of me. Is this your new look? Because I kind of like it."

"You do not," Hamilton says, dusting the flour off one of his shoulders. "I look ridiculous."

"Did you do this to yourself?" I ask, and Hamilton sighs.

"Obviously not. Piper is working on a series of makeup tutorials based on characters from books or movies, and she doesn't want to be the only model or people will think her channel is just for girls."

"I'm not sure she's at the level to be tutoring anyone," I say as I take a seat on the step.

"You were very kind to help her practice," Marjorie says as she reaches over to rub her thumb across his cheek. "Is this…?"

"Flour," Hamilton repeats as he turns to pick up his backpack.

"Wait," I say, jumping to my feet. "A makeup tutorial? You mean for her YouTube channel? You're on YouTube? Like this?"

Marjorie's eyes grow, and Hamilton hangs his head. "Sweetie, are you on YouTube? You know my policy about social media."

Hamilton shakes his head. "I know. Parental approval

before any photo or video uploads. She hasn't posted it yet. She has to edit it first."

"You're going to let her put it up?" I'm shocked that he agreed to this in the first place, let alone to have it all over the internet.

"I'll talk to her dad tomorrow at school," Marjorie offers, and Hamilton shakes his head.

"It's not a big deal, Mom. No one watches her channel anyway." He grabs his backpack from the floor. "Can I go shower now or do you two need some more time to laugh at me?"

"Of course, sweetie," Marjorie says, giving him a pat on the back. "I'll bring up some of my makeup remover. You'll need it."

~

Thirty minutes later, I knock on Hamilton's door, Marjorie having extended our Quiet Time to accommodate for Hamilton's transformation.

"It's open," he yells, and I poke my head in to see if he's in a mood to talk. He's sitting on his bed, his damp hair still slumped to the side, his lips now a shade of blue. He's fiddling with a Rubik's Cube, his hands moving with the mastery of a pianist.

"It's alive!" I say, and he gives me a look, his fingers

still flying. Apparently, he isn't ready for jokes. Since he doesn't ask me to leave, I decide to tell him. Maybe the news, even bad news, will take his mind off the black glitter still clinging to his scalp.

"Did you get any news at Crossroads?" Hamilton asks, beating me to it.

"Not good news."

"What happened?" He scoots over on the edge of his bed, making room for me. I take a seat on the floor instead.

"She's still going to the Nickersons'. Everything's set for her to move in Thursday."

"Geez, this Thursday?" Hamilton asks, and I nod. He wipes a drip off his cheek. A sparkle lingers next to a freckle. "Also, it seems like a broken system if foster parent drug abuse isn't a big enough problem. We should call the news or something. They could go undercover, a special edition report: Inside Foster Homes—Joy or... I don't know any drug names that start with *j*."

"I don't know what happened. Maybe they have problems with their computers...."

"Happiness or Hallucinogens."

"That's not really our biggest..."

"Love or LSD."

I whack Hamilton on the knee. "Enough with the

weird drug mottoes. We made up the whole drug thing anyway, remember?"

"Right. What *is* the problem with the Bad Family?"

"It doesn't matter."

"Yes, it does. Obviously. Drugs weren't enough to push CPS into action. Was it worse than drugs? Was there…murder? You can tell me!"

"I'll tell you when you need to know, and right now, you don't need to know."

"Can you just confirm it's not murder? I don't feel mature enough to handle murder."

"No murder."

"Whew."

I grab the Rubik's Cube out of his hand and begin finishing the other half. Hamilton pulls his tiny reporter's notebook out of his back pocket. He flips through a couple of pages before stopping on one.

"Make call to Child Protective Services using a teen with an adult voice to impersonate neighbor. Fail." He crosses out the line. "Plan Number Two…So what's Plan Number Two? Or Operation Number Two? 'Operation' sounds more official, but a little too soldiery for what we're doing."

I fiddle with the drawstring of the tie-dyed pajama pants Marjorie bought me for my birthday last year. I can't meet his eyes because our biggest problem is that I don't have a Plan Number Two.

Hamilton flips back in his notebook. "Plan Number One's objective was to keep Meridee away from the Bad Family by ensuring the Bad Family is seen as bad so they can't take her in."

I keep listening.

"If our ultimate goal is to keep Meridee away from the Bad Family, then…" He reaches over and plucks the Rubik's Cube from my lap. He mumbles that same line about our ultimate goal over and over to himself as his fingers pick up speed. The colored blocks move and twist and turn until finally a full side is yellow and he stops. "We need to get her a better family! If our ultimate goal is to keep Meridee away from the Bad Family, then we just need to find her a better family. Then she won't have to go there, because this better family can take her!"

He fist-pumps, lunging into the air slightly before falling back on his bed, the pillows bouncing beside him.

"Shh!" I warn. "Or your mom is going to remember it's past our Quiet Time and send us to our rooms."

"This is brilliant! I'm brilliant!" he whispers, making a snow angel on the comforter.

"Hold on, Einstein," I say, pulling his hand so he's sitting upright. "A better family would be great, but that's not how it works. They don't rate families. How would that be fair? You're a precious angel, so you get a ten family. You're a delinquent with acne and bad test scores, you get a four!"

Hamilton frowns. "I didn't think about that."

"You don't know how it works."

"It could still be an idea. You said that these people don't even like kids, right? So maybe we get someone who wants her more. And then it's not like she's going to a better family, it's that she's going to someone who really wants her."

"I guess..."

Emboldened by the fact that I didn't immediately say no, Hamilton continues. "We just need to get someone to meet her. Do they have, like, a time when parents can come to Crossroads and meet kids?"

"They do, but those things don't happen often and she wouldn't get to go since she already has a placement. It's still possible she'll end up back with her mom in the long run, so we just need a family for right now."

Hamilton flops back on the bed. "This is giving me a headache!" He massages his temples with his fingers. "Maybe I'm actually sick, which would be great because I wouldn't have to do my performance test tomorrow in band. And if I was sick, I could stay home and think of a plan. I really wish I had a hint of the flu or something so I wouldn't have to go."

Suddenly, it hits me.

"If you were sick, you wouldn't have to go!"

"I'd have to be really sick, though, with a measurable temperature, or Mom will just send me with throat lozenges." Hamilton puts a hand to his head. "Maybe I do feel warm, but it could just be the shower."

"You're not sick," I say as Marjorie nears the door. "But you did just give me an idea for a new plan!"

"Seriously? What is it?"

"Shhh," I say as I hear Marjorie's feet on the stairs. "Quiet Time is over."

Hamilton lunges across the bed for his notebook. "But what do I write down for the plan?"

"You can call it Operation Home Sick. I'll give you the details tomorrow."

As I open the door to Hamilton's room, I feel my stomach settle. His fake illness may have cured mine. It may even save Meridee.

# APPENDICITIS

The next day, I skip out of fourth period and head to the lunchroom, determined to find Santos and tell him the new plan. We don't need him to help this time, but I want him to know that I appreciate what he did. And to remind him that he doesn't owe me supplies.

The A lunch period is packed with a lot of eighth graders, and I follow a group of students through the main door, keeping my head down as I pass Ms. Taylor, the only person likely to notice me. Once the other students begin splitting into the different lunch lines, I search for Santos. I scan the recycling, garbage, and compost bins where another group of detention-serving students stand in aprons and latex gloves, waiting to help students sort the slop on their trays into the appropriate bin.

Since Santos is not working the refuse station, he must be serving, and I look at the growing lines of students flowing out three separate doors. I decide to join Line Two. Thankfully, the line is moving faster than expected, and it's not long before I'm enveloped in the smell of hot grease. I stand up on my tiptoes to peer into the food station, but the only person I can see is Mike, the adult cafeteria assistant. Without a word, a short kid passes me an empty tray, almost hitting me in the stomach. I forgot about this part. That I'd actually have to get a lunch. I spot Santos at the end of the line, a hairnet pulled over his hood. I detect a single earbud and smile at his guts. Here he is serving detention and still, he's out of dress code.

I say yes to each item I'm offered by the depressed student servers even though I can't eat any of it now. It does bother me a little, to waste food. Maybe I can hand it off to some hungry kid in the cafeteria, since the school doesn't offer seconds. I try to make eye contact with Santos as I move closer to him, but he stubbornly keeps his head down as he slides paper cups of ketchup or mustard across the counter. Finally, he looks up and spots me. He doesn't smile, I was expecting that, but his mouth twitches in a way I know he sees me. He slides a ketchup cup to a girl in a pink jacket.

"It didn't work," I mouth as I sidestep closer to him. He nods, passes another ketchup cup, and now I'm only three students away.

"But I have a new plan," I whisper when our eyes meet again, and he raises an eyebrow, intrigued.

"What?" he mouths back, and I give him a look that says, "Give me a sec." Unless he's a master lip reader, there's no way I can communicate my brilliance in the lunch line. Santos looks over at Ilene, the cafeteria supervisor, who is methodically plopping hamburgers or hot dogs into the waiting buns. Her tight ringlets are growing in the steam, escaping through the holes of her hairnet.

Santos grabs the edges of the ketchup and mustard tray before giving me a nod and turning to a little closet behind him. Grabbing my tray, I follow him to the closet, where he is lining up white cups on a fresh tray.

"So?" he asks, pumping the handle of a large ketchup tub, never spilling a drop of the red goo.

"It didn't work. Lenny said she's moving in tomorrow, so either they didn't investigate or they didn't find anything."

"Guess we shouldn't have said drugs."

"Drugs could have worked."

"They didn't."

"I'm aware of that fact," I say, now wondering why I even bothered to tell him if he was going to be such a jerk.

"What's the new plan?" He's moved on to the mustard.

I smile, because while my first plan didn't work, this one is brilliant.

"Appendicitis."

"What?"

"She's going to fake an appendicitis attack on Thursday night when she gets there. They'll have to take her to the hospital to check it out. It's not a long-term solution, obviously, but it buys me a couple of days to think of something else."

Santos is silent while he pumps mustard into the next row of cups. Suddenly, a small smile creeps across his face. "I shoulda done that."

"I know, right? I was sick when I showed up to my first house, but it wasn't bad enough. I researched and found appendicitis. It has to be something she could go to the hospital for."

"She's just gonna fake it?"

"I'll have to teach her what to do, the symptoms and everything, but if she gets it right, she could pull it off."

"She should go to Saint David's," Santos says as he lays out a few more white paper cups. "The caseworker, Ms. Casey, is cool. She gets in your business, makes you write about your feelings and stuff like that, but—"

"Hey! You! What are you doing back here?" a voice booms behind me, and I turn to see one of the cooks with her hands on her hips, sweat dripping along her bandanna-covered hairline. "You don't have proper cafeteria service attire."

"I'm leaving," I say as I grab my tray, hoping she wasn't loud enough to alert an administrator. I'm glad she doesn't have a walkie-talkie to radio them.

"And you? Get that hoodie off your head and put that hairnet right!"

I stop at the door, looking back to see Santos smiling at me. He grabs the tray and heads back to the line, pausing first to secure his earbud underneath his hairnet.

## OUCH

That afternoon, Hamilton makes his first trip to Crossroads. He thinks it looks like a prison for kids—and he's not wrong. The colorless buildings, the chain-link fence, the faded swing set with rusted poles don't look welcoming, but it didn't feel that way. Inside, we find Meridee sitting on the dingy white carpet in the playroom, surrounded by the mountain of limbless Barbies. I wave at the few kids I know, taking note of those I don't recognize so I can come back and set up their first consultations. We crouch down at the edge of the ring of Barbies, but Meridee doesn't look up. It's too loud in here for her to have noticed we've gotten so close.

"It looks like a Mattel massacre in here," Hamilton whispers, and I lose my balance, slamming my hand down on the heel of a tiny Barbie shoe.

"Ow!"

Meridee's head snaps up. "Are you okay?"

I examine the tiny red point in the center of my palm. "Just a small scratch."

"Do you want me to high-five it?"

"You mean kiss it?" Hamilton says, now sitting on his knees beside me.

Meridee screws up her face, shaking her head. "No kisses. Just high fives."

"Sure," I say, putting my hand toward her. "You can high-five it."

She gently slaps her small palm into mine, more of a soft press than a true high five, but it does make me feel a little better.

"Who are you?" Meridee asks Hamilton as she attempts to shove some stiff Barbie legs into the seat of a pink convertible.

"This is Hamilton. I live at his house."

"Is he your brother?"

I smile, surprised that she doesn't notice the difference between Hamilton's pale, freckled skin and mine. "Sort of."

"You can call me Hambone," Hamilton says as he clears himself a seat in the Barbie gear. I'm surprised at his sweetness. I've never seen him with younger kids before.

"You be Nicki," Meridee tells him as she plops a half-dressed Barbie into Hamilton's palm.

Hamilton looks puzzled as he twists the Barbie in his hand. "Whoa!" he shouts as her head falls onto the floor. Then, again whispering to me, "These toys are a living nightmare!" I take the decapitated doll from him. We have work to do.

"Actually, Meridee, we're here to teach you a new game! Do you want to play?"

"It's soooo fun!" Hamilton adds, and Meridee looks at both of us with a raised eyebrow.

"I want to play Barbies."

"You can play Barbies when we're done, but this game is so fun!"

She shakes her head, the multicolored barrettes clinking in her hair.

"I think it's time," Hamilton whispers.

"We hardly tried yet."

"You're the one who said we needed to work fast."

"Fine," I say, shaking my head and twisting my backpack around so I can reach into the front pocket.

Out I pull six fruity Tootsie Rolls, the mini kind they throw off floats during parades.

"Meridee," I say, shaking the candies in my palm. "Did you know if you play our fun game you can win prizes?"

I hold out the sweets like a hand full of gold, and her eyes widen at the sight of sugar. Just like me. She abandons the convertible with the Barbie dangling out the side door.

"You only get one if you play," Hamilton encourages, and she nods her head, scooting toward us.

"Okay!" I tell her, closing the candies in my hand and hopping to my feet. "But we have to play outside. Come on."

Outside, we find a spot in the empty playground, taking a seat in the grass near the old swing set the kids aren't supposed to use because the poles come out of the ground if you swing too high. Hamilton and I match Meridee's cross-legged seat, and I spread out the candies in the center of our circle.

"One…two…three…four…five…six!" Meridee counts, and we applaud, already acting like proud parents.

"So this game is called Ouch," I explain as Meridee eyes the pink pieces of joy. "It's only for special kids like you! Hamilton—"

"Hambone," Meridee interrupts.

"Yes, Hambone is going to do something and then you repeat after him. Kind of like Simon Says."

Beside me, Hamilton has his notebook flat on the ground and is reviewing the notes we took today in the library during lunch. He mouths the words, making small cringing facial gestures as he reads. He was better at the gestures than me, so we chose him to be the actor, me the director.

"Ready, Hambone?"

He nods, his face serious.

"First, do you know where your belly button is?" he asks, and Meridee nods, pointing her finger into the belly of her striped shirt.

"That's right! So, first you put your hand on your belly button and you do this." Hamilton bites his lip, squeezing the edges of his mouth together like he's playing the clarinet, and squints his eyes. "Oooh."

"Do you think you can do that?" I ask Meridee, and she nods, her face already beginning to mimic Hamilton's. This might actually work.

"Oh," says Meridee with the same lip bite, but her eyes are completely closed. Hamilton and I applaud, and I hand her the first candy. She'll need to do better than that, but I want to encourage her for trying.

"Do it again," I instruct Hamilton, and he repeats the action three times, pausing between each motion. Meridee watches him as she chomps her Tootsie Roll. I pocket the wrapper and find myself biting my lip and squinting my eyes, too.

"Watch me," Hamilton says, scooting closer to her in the grass. "First you bite your lip just a little bit and then close your eyes a tiny bit, like you're looking at the sun and it's too bright."

Her tiny face twists to match his; I wish I had a camera phone.

"Oooh," they say together, and I applaud. Hamilton breaks into a big grin.

"Okay, I think she's got the first one. Let's try the next one and we can come back," he says as he grabs the notebook.

We spend the next fifteen minutes walking Meridee through the steps of an appendix attack, knowing it will be difficult to make it not look like a regular old stomachache. We teach her to rub her temples with a headache, and Hamilton shows her how to move her stomach pain from her belly button to her lower right abdomen, using her small palm to measure the distance. With a press on the area, we show her how to flinch over the "rebound tenderness" when someone quickly pushes on the part of her stomach we just found. Together, they blow their cheeks out like an inflated blowfish before they groan, "I'm gonna vomit!" Back and forth they repeat the motions with me cheering and unwrapping candies, moving from tiny Tootsie Rolls to miniature Snickers bars to, finally, the round, rainbow-colored lollipop that now fills her mouth and spreads across her cheeks.

"I think I'm actually going to be sick," Hamilton says as he flops back on the grass, his arms flung above his head, his eyes closed. "But she's got it."

Meridee crawls over to Hamilton and peers down at his face, a dangle of purple-and-pink saliva threatening to drip onto his cheek.

"Hambone." She giggles, moving her face closer to his. "Wake up!"

He opens one eye to look at her. "I'm not sleeping; I'm just appendixed out."

"Let him rest a minute," I tell Meridee, leaning over to gently pull her arm toward me. "We'll be back tomorrow and you can play some more. Remember, though, you can't tell anyone about the game yet. It's a surprise."

Meridee doesn't acknowledge me, absorbed instead by her attempt to peel off the sticky plastic protecting the rest of her lollipop.

"Meridee, did you hear me? Don't tell anyone yet. It's a surprise for tomorrow."

"I know!" she yells, and I realize she must be getting tired, too.

I wonder if she knows what is going to happen tomorrow. Is she still young enough to be moved around without any information? Does she know when she'll get to see her mom again? Does she hope with every open door that it will be her mom walking into the room?

"We should go now," I tell Hamilton, who is still in starfish position in the browning grass. "They're going to come get her for dinner soon, and we don't want them to see all of this."

I gesture to the candy wrapper debris surrounding us. Hamilton groans as he lifts himself up, closing his notebook and tucking it into his back pocket before helping me collect the garbage. I hand him the small Ziploc bag I brought for this purpose while I get a wet wipe to clean up the destruction I knew would occur on Meridee's face.

"Here, Meridee," I say as I hand her the wipe. "You've gotta clean your face a little bit."

"I'm sticky!" she squeals as she rubs her face, smearing the sugar rather than cleaning it.

"Ready?" Hamilton asks as he hands me the Ziploc of candy wrappers.

"For tonight, at least." I slide on my backpack before standing up and brushing the grass off my pants. The sun is beginning to pinken behind the buildings, changing their color from a dull gray to a warm rose. As I walk toward the house, I notice Meridee slip her sticky hand into Hamilton's. He squeezes hers a bit tighter.

"Hambone," she says quietly.

"We'll be back tomorrow," he says.

"With more candy?"

"With more candy," I repeat. We'll be back, determined to keep her as happy as she is right now, her stomach full of sugar, her hand held.

# THE GOTHS DESCEND

The next morning, Hamilton and I are silent in the car on the way to school. Marjorie glances at herself in the rearview mirror, practicing for her new podcast on being a single foster mom. Normally, Hamilton would be giving her notes, but today we're both focused on Meridee. We told Marjorie we would be staying late to work on a project for science, though we'll rush to Crossroads when the last bell rings to see Meridee before she gets dropped off at the Nickersons'. In our backpacks is the homework we haphazardly finished, neither of us feeling the energy to complete the bonus problems. Who cares about getting an A when someone's life is about to collapse?

I'm chewing the ends of my hair, running through the checklist for our meeting with Meridee, when I see it. It's just a flash, but I swear I saw black-glittered hair and dark eyeliner. I tap Hamilton's shoulder to point out the student when we pull up to the curb, and there they are: a handful of students dressed in their typical T-shirts and shorts, but with gothic heads, hair combed over one eye with black glitter holding it in place. Two boys have identical black eyeliner while another girl has turned her black eyeliner into polka dots around her eyes.

"Hamilton...," I whisper as Marjorie reaches the drop-off spot. He's busy stuffing something in his bag and doesn't lift his head until he hears Marjorie's "Oh my." He sits speechless, taking a moment to adjust his glasses on his nose before leaning closer to the window.

"That certainly can't be dress code," Marjorie says.

"There are no restrictions for hairstyles or personal grooming in the dress code." Hamilton's voice is expressionless as he continues to stare out the window.

"I take it people watched your video," I say as the car behind us honks.

"You two better get going," Marjorie says, and we hustle to grab our lunch things. His eyes are still on the goths milling around the flagpole as he kisses his mom good-bye.

"Have a great day, Pav!" Marjorie yells out the window. I can't hear what she says to Hamilton, but I don't bother to listen, since I've spotted Piper bouncing up and down at the edge of the curb. Hamilton hangs his head as he moves around the front of the car, not even looking up as Piper shouts his name. Before we get to the sidewalk, she is off the curb and running toward us, immediately grabbing Hamilton's hands.

"Get back on the sidewalk!" the crosswalk monitor yells, and Piper gives the officer a snooty look before yanking Hamilton to her spot by the flagpole.

"Four hundred twenty-three views!" she shouts, lifting their clasped hands above her head. "Can you believe it? That's almost half the school! I've never had above fifty, and now we're famous!"

She pulls him into a huge bear hug, pinning his arms at his side.

"We have to do another video! I wish I had brought my black lipstick so we could get in on the trend. This is just so…ahhhh!" She pulls Hamilton into another hug.

He still looks shocked and keeps adjusting his glasses and squinting at the kids around him as if he can't be seeing right. Piper steps in front of him, setting herself up as a bouncer, preventing the flow of kids beginning to line up. "I love your video!" they shout, and Piper beams.

"Check out SparkleGirl285 for more videos!" Piper reaches out to shake the hands stretched out toward Hamilton. "More tutorials are on the way!"

"Are you okay?" I ask, and Hamilton looks like he doesn't see me before a huge smile spreads across his face.

"Sure...I guess Goth Boy has a special appeal I don't normally possess."

I thought he'd be embarrassed, but as the bell rings, he adjusts his glasses one more time and then steps into the waiting mob. I follow a few feet behind him, joining the crush of students headed toward the open doors.

"No. Flour," I hear him tell a girl whose face is streaked with what must be face paint. She looks like a skeleton, her brown eyes surrounded by charcoal eye shadow. At the door, he turns back to me and offers a thumbs-up.

"See you at lunch!" he shouts, and I return the thumbs-up, a weight dropping into my stomach. I hope Goth Boy doesn't forget he still needs to be Hambone.

~

By the time seventh period arrives, I've had enough of the fake goth crowd. Thankfully, no one in class is wearing any black, though one girl's lips are a strange shade of gray. At the door, Mr. Ramirez gives high fives in his tweed vest and olive-green bow tie. I sort of expect him to start speaking with a British accent. He did that once last year for an entire week. I scribble my response to today's warm-up as the seats fill up around me, but everyone leaves the one beside me empty. The countdown timer runs on the whiteboard; Hamilton only has about thirty seconds before he's late. He's never late.

"You better run," Mr. Ramirez suddenly says, his voice booming down the hallway over the ringing bell. Hamilton and Piper barrel into the classroom, causing Mr. Ramirez to jump back. Winded, they both bend over with their hands on their knees, their gasping breaths almost synced to the beat of the piano pop songs Mr. Ramirez often plays. There's a hint of black in Hamilton's hair.

"We're here," Piper shouts, raising Hamilton's hand above their heads like he's a champion boxer.

"That's Goth Boy," someone whispers, and Piper beams, turning Hamilton side to side with his hand still above her head.

"That timer is going!" Mr. Ramirez barks, and our heads drop while our pencils start to fly. I add to my answer, not lifting my head as Hamilton takes the seat beside me, his breathing still heavy. I flick my eyes to him and notice the smudged black nail polish on his fingers.

"Look at me quick," Piper whispers to Hamilton from the desk across from him. She pops her finger into her mouth and leans toward Hamilton's face.

"It's fine. Just leave it," he says, jerking back, keeping his eyes on the question on the board.

"I just need to fix this...."

"We can get it after school," he whispers, his attention now back on his paper. Mr. Ramirez stares at Hamilton with a raised eyebrow as he logs our attendance into the computer. I wonder if he will give Hamilton and Piper tardies. Probably not. Hamilton can get away with just about anything at this school. Probably because he stays after class to help teachers tidy up. He can't keep his own room clean, but he won't leave a classroom without pushing in all the chairs.

"You decided to return to Goth Boy, huh?"

Hamilton glances over, his pencil still moving. "I got kinda swept up."

"Fame can do that to you."

"It's not...," he starts, but the timer cuts him off. I look him over while Mr. Ramirez collects our warm-ups. Hamilton's look is a messier version of the night of the video. The glitter isn't smoothed into each strand, but speckled across his head. The eyeliner looks like Cleopatra on one side and is barely noticeable on the other. No flour on his face, though he does look paler than usual. This must be why he stood me up at lunch.

As we start class, I'm grateful we're doing independent work, because I don't feel like working with Goth Boy. Unfortunately, Piper ignores the zero-voice requirement for independent work and continues a stream of whispered conversation.

"We really need to capitalize on this attention and make another video," she explains to Hamilton, clearly loud enough so I can hear, too. "I've been thinking about a cartoon makeup tutorial where you make someone look like a cartoon character; I saw it done on a couple channels...."

"So, you're going to copy someone else's tutorial?" I ask.

Piper glares at me, tapping her lime-green pen on her desk. "No. They're just inspiration. I'll add my own personality."

"And Hamilton's. He's the only reason people are watching your channel."

Piper's glossed lips pop open in a gasp, and Hamilton turns to me with a frown.

"Piper does all the editing and concept development. There'd be no Goth Boy without her."

"And what would the world do without Goth Boy?" I don't know why I'm being so mean, but I can't stop myself.

Mr. Ramirez's sudden presence near our desks stops our conversation, but Hamilton's hurt lingers. We each go back to our double bubble map comparing and contrasting Stephen F. Austin with Sam Houston, but it's not even thirty seconds before Piper is off again.

"Goth Boy is great, so we could do variations on his look. Maybe day versus night for Goth Boy? Or Goth Boy Glam for prom or something?"

"Or Goth Boy Golden Glow for his days at the beach....Oh wait, Goth Boy doesn't sunbathe," I say mockingly. "How'd he deal with a tan?"

Piper chooses to ignore me. So does Hamilton.

"Can you come over tonight?" Piper asks, doodling a rainbow on the edge of her paper. "We can pick up some makeup from Target after school and then shoot the video. It'll be great! My dad can order pizza. Do you want to use my phone to text your mom?" She digs around in her backpack for the phone she isn't supposed to have at school.

"Well…I don't know about tonight," Hamilton says, his eyes darting to me. "Maybe tomorrow?"

"It has to be tonight, or we'll lose the attention."

"It's just…," Hamilton says, his face pained, as he clearly wants to say yes. I decide to end his problems for him.

"Film it tonight," I say.

"But it's our last chance to practice with Meridee," Hamilton whispers, leaning closer to me so Piper can't hear.

"Practice what?" she asks, leaning over, too.

"I can do it." I add another circle to my map. "She's ready to go. And Piper's right. You don't want to lose the attention."

"But I want to…"

"Just make your video, Goth Boy. Your fans need you."

I focus on my paper, surprised by the tingling wetness at the corners of my eyes.

"Hamilton. Pavi. Piper. You three need to find new seats." Mr. Ramirez sighs as he walks toward us.

"But we weren't even talking," Piper whines, and Mr. Ramirez gives her the look of every teacher who's been challenged on something so obvious: tilted head, lips pursed as if to say, "Really? *Really?*"

Mr. Ramirez drops our lyrics project onto the center

of our desks. The glaring purple 82 stares at all of us, the happy-go-lucky color not making me feel any better than if it was red ink. It's worse seeing it in person.

"I'm not moving, since I wasn't the one talking last," Piper says as she glares at me. "And I wasn't in charge of typing that project, so, really, that shouldn't be reflected in my grade."

"It's called a group project for a reason. Group work. Group grade." Mr. Ramirez folds his arms across his chest. "And I don't care who moves as long as you each find seats where you can be productive."

I pick up my papers, not having the energy to argue.

"I'm going to come with you," Hamilton says as I stand up and push in my chair.

"Don't worry about it. I'll be fine on my own."

I find an empty desk in the front of the room, underneath the old TV that looks like it could fall off the wall and squash me at any second. Hamilton sits down beside the girl with gray lipstick, and Piper preens from the desk she never left. I catch Hamilton's eye for a second before turning to my notebook and the practically empty bubble map.

I can do this alone. I can do all of it alone.

# FINAL PREPARATIONS

The bus stinks. Everyone inside is varying levels of damp due to the light sprinkling outside. The heater being used for the first time this season makes it smell like old closet. I can feel my temperature rising as I sit crammed between two elderly ladies in puffy coats that are meant for the snow we'll never see here. I sprinted to the bus stop after school, and now my sweaty stink adds to the garbage-dump mixture of the bus. Thankfully, I'll be at Crossroads in a couple of blocks.

I lean my head back against the window, the metal edge cutting into my neck. Meridee is going to ask for Hambone. She'll want to know where he is, why he didn't come to play Ouch with her. She's already without her mom, and soon she'll leave her new Crossroads friends. Now she has to lose Hambone, too? I knew I shouldn't have let him help. My clients have serious problems and can't be dropped the minute something better comes along.

And it's not like I needed him anyway: I made the plan. I researched all the symptoms and their correct order. Haven't I learned anything from years of being on my own? If you want it done well, you've got to do it yourself. If you want it done at all, even badly, you have to do it yourself. You're on your own. I can't believe I let myself think otherwise.

At my stop, I mutter a thank-you to the driver, grateful the rain has cleared and the sun is starting to break through the gray clouds. I wait for the bus to move before crossing the street, a lesson I learned in one of my first Crossroads workshops on independence. Once an older man finds the right change, the doors close and the bus rumbles past, splashing gutter water onto my shoes.

Then I see him. Across the street, standing beside the chain-link fence is Hamilton, his backpack and his baritone beside him.

"Pavi. Sharma. Get over here!" Hamilton stands with one hand on his hip, the other pointing down at the sidewalk beside him. I look both ways before crossing toward him, keeping my head down, since I'm not ready to make eye contact. Up close, his face is red like a cartoon character ready to blow steam out of its ears. He drops his arms to his sides and stares at me, a dark cloud brewing behind those red glasses.

"Did you walk here?" I ask, and he rolls his eyes, something I've never seen him do before. The movement is even more dramatic with his eyes lined in black.

"How would I have beaten you here on foot? Piper's dad gave me a ride, though he didn't really want to drop me off in this part of town. I told him I was doing community service."

"What about Piper's video?"

"What ABOUT Piper's video?" Hamilton shouts, his hands flying into the air like a symphony conductor signaling the first note. "You turned that stupid video into this huge deal, and for what? Nothing! Yes, I made a video that became popular. Yes, I enjoyed my celebrity status for the afternoon. Yes, I agreed to let Piper put waterproof makeup on me in the bathroom during lunch and now I might be having a slight allergic reaction, but that doesn't matter because I am not a bad guy for having fun!"

He takes a deep breath and adjusts his glasses.

"You didn't—" I try, but he cuts me off.

"And it is NOT okay for you to just kick me out of this operation, because it is not a real company and you are not a real boss, so you can't fire me! Also, I didn't even do anything to compromise the state of the mission! This is my project, too, and you can't just tell me not to be a part of it. You don't get to do it by yourself! I am here and I am going to help Meridee as Goth Boy or as Hambone, but it doesn't matter what she calls me, because what matters is her! And teaching her to properly fake the symptoms of appendicitis! So, no more telling me I'm out. Got it?"

Stunned, I only manage to nod.

"Now, let's get in there and make this girl sick!"

Hamilton slugs his backpack over his shoulders and grabs the baritone by the middle, bending his knees to lift it up. He takes one step before bumping into the closed gate.

"Let me help you," I say as I slide past him, opening the gate and grabbing the bottom of the baritone. Together, we move to the front entry, resting the baritone on the step as I open the main door.

The front office is quiet again. I lean over the counter and see a half-drunk cup of coffee and two leftover bites of a Snickers bar atop a stack of manila folders. Lenny must be here somewhere. I am in no mood to talk to him.

"Hey there, Pav," Lenny says as he rounds the corner, a large cardboard box obscuring his face. I grab his coffee cup and the Snickers bar from the desk before he plops the box down on top of the folders. "Thanks!"

He tosses the last piece of candy in his mouth, chomping away as he sorts through the box of papers. Hamilton is trying to hide behind the edge of the wall, rubbing at the black eyeliner.

"Hey, man, who're you?" Lenny leans around the edge of the counter, and I realize he hasn't met Hamilton yet. We don't have time for them to get to know each other, or for Hamilton to begin his barrage of questions, so I quickly take over.

"This is my foster brother, Hamilton...."

"Nice to meet you."

"So you live with Pavi, huh? Hopefully she doesn't boss you around too much?"

"Saying 'bossy' is antigirl, but she does like things done right, especially when it comes to her busi—"

"We need to get home before the rain really starts," I say as I step behind Hamilton, placing my hands on his shoulders and directing him to the hallway door. "Can you buzz us through so we can see Meridee? I want to say good-bye before she goes tonight."

Lenny gives me a strange look. "I didn't know you knew her that well."

"I've been spending some time with her. I remember my first time in the shelter."

Lenny nods, his face softening. Foster care words affect shelter staff, too.

"Can we leave this here?" I say, gesturing toward the baritone, and Lenny nods.

"Whatever you need, Pav."

The door buzzes, and I reach past Hamilton to turn the knob and push it open.

"Nice look, man," Lenny says to Hamilton.

"Thanks! You can find the tutorial at SparkleGirl—" I shove Hamilton before he can finish, closing the door behind me. "Thanks for making me seem like an anti-social weirdo," Hamilton says as he wriggles out of my grasp. "I didn't even get to explain all this." He swirls his palm in front of his face.

"Let Goth Boy's look speak for itself. We don't have time to talk. Her caseworker will be here to get her soon."

We don't find Meridee in the playroom or in the den. I leave Hamilton on the back steps while I run across to see if she's in the girls' dorms. I search the rooms, even checking under the twin bed frames in case she's using an escape I tried, too. My heart starts to accelerate when I don't find her in the bathroom or in the closets. I hope we're not too late.

"She's not in there," I yell as I return to the backyard. Hamilton's sitting on the step, Meridee standing below him so she's eye level. As I walk toward them, Meridee scans Hamilton's face, her nose centimeters from his skin, her mouth in tight consideration. She delicately picks up a glittered strand of clumped hairs, holding it away from Hamilton's head before letting it fall. She lets out a giggle.

"You look weird, Hambone."

Hamilton laughs. "That's okay. Weird is good."

She squats down and looks up at him. "Weird is weird."

"Weird is wonderful," Hamilton says as he leans toward her, googling his eyes and sticking out his tongue. She giggles and reaches out to touch his pale cheeks.

"Okay, you two weirdos. We don't have long, and we need to play Ouch one more time."

"Do you have candy?" Meridee asks, and I nod. She races ahead to the grass by the swing set, and Hamilton and I hurry to follow her, taking a seat in the same circle we made yesterday. The grass is still damp, but we don't have time to worry about that. Without pulling out his notebook, Hamilton starts going through the symptoms, giving subtle corrections and adjustments like a sculptor perfecting his masterpiece.

"Eyes closed a little more," he corrects. "Hands a little lower on your belly."

Meridee repeats each of his moves, occasionally reaching out to squeeze his hand before sitting back in the grass. Together they frown and groan, holding their stomachs and tilting their heads back in mock pain. She looks good. She can actually pull this off.

After twenty minutes of practice, I realize it's time. I swallow back the guilt that fills my throat as I think about what I am going to say next.

"Okay, Meridee. That was great." I hand her the last Tootsie Roll and watch her sticky fingers twist the ends of the wrapper, dropping the candy into her palm. "Remember how tonight you're going to sleep somewhere else? At a new house?"

Meridee frowns. "I want to go home."

"I know you do. And do you know how you get to go home?"

She shakes her head sadly. I give her a cheerleader smile.

"I do! Do you want to learn how to do it?"

She pops to her knees, nodding her head like the bobblehead Jane Austen on Marjorie's front dash.

"The lady who comes to see you sometimes is going to come here and take you to the new house. You're going to be really quiet and put your hands on your tummy. You're going to get ready to play Ouch, but you can't get started until you get out of the car, okay? That's the rules."

"That's the rules," she repeats, looking over at Hamilton.

"That's the rules," he echoes.

"And when you get to the new house, you're going to play Ouch but all by yourself. Do you know what things to do first?"

She nods, putting her hands on her stomach and groaning slightly, her eyes squinting. After a few seconds, she breaks into a huge grin.

"Good, good," I tell her, and Hamilton gives her a high five. "The lady isn't going to do Ouch like Hambone; she's going to play by saying, 'Are you sick, Meridee?'" I do my best old-lady voice and she laughs. I shouldn't make her laugh. She has to be serious. "And when she asks you, then you do the next step of Ouch. Do you know the next one?"

She blows out her cheeks, lunging over as if she's about to puke. When she brings her head up, she lets her lip hang heavy, her brow furrowed. "I'm gonna vomit."

"We should have taught her to say 'throw up' instead of 'vomit,'" Hamilton whispers. "What kid says 'vomit'?"

"Too late now." I give Meridee a huge smile and a thumbs-up.

"She wants you to stay at the new house, but you just keep playing Ouch until you're back in the car. Then she's gonna take you to the hospital and it will be so fun there! You'll get Jell-O and special pajamas!"

"Red Jell-O?"

"Yeah!" I say.

"I love Jell-O!"

"Me too!" I continue. "And once you get to the hospital, then you can stop playing Ouch. Nice nurses are going to come see you, and then you say you feel better, okay? You don't play Ouch anymore, okay? You DO NOT play Ouch in the hospital."

"Got it, Meridee?" Hamilton says, leaning toward her. "You play Ouch in the car and at the house but not. At. The hospital."

"Where do you play Ouch?" I ask again.

"At the car and the house!"

"Yes," I say. "And where do you never, ever, ever play Ouch?"

"At the hospital!"

We all cheer, Meridee looking back and forth between us to take in our approval.

"And if you play right, Ouch in the car and at the house, and no more Ouch at the hospital, then…" I take a deep breath, feeling awful about what I'm going to say next. "Then you'll get to stay with Mama again. But she won't come if you don't play right."

I force myself to look at the fear in her eyes, feeling tears spring into mine. I remember that desire, the overwhelming panic that I would never see Ma's face again. I try to swallow. This is something I had to do. I would never, never say this to a regular client, but she can't make a mistake tonight.

"So you have to play right, okay?"

Meridee nods. I grab my backpack and set it in my lap. Meridee leans forward to watch me unzip the top pocket. I pull out a small red sock with lace trim around the top.

"This is for you," I tell Meridee, and she scrunches up her nose.

"You're giving her a sock?" Hamilton asks.

"It's a lucky sock. I had it when I was a little girl and it helped me be safe, so I want you to have it." I reach in my backpack and pull out the more practical gifts I have. "Here's some granola bars and some fruit snacks."

I don't know what she'll eat when she gets to the Nickersons'. No one ever made dinner for me when I lived there. Most times he'd leave different boxes of cereal on the counter and a carton of milk in the fridge. Sometimes it smelled a little sour, and I would eat the cereal plain, tossing it into my mouth like popcorn.

I tuck the snacks into the sock, stretching it out so that it will never fit her tiny foot. The sole is already threadbare from the years I actually wore it. I've kept it in my pillowcase every night since, an embarrassing security sock to help me fall asleep. It smelled like home for a long time. It doesn't anymore.

"It's time for us to go now," I tell Meridee as I zip up my backpack and sling it over my shoulders. Hamilton rushes to stand up beside me, and for a second, Meridee sits below us, looking smaller than she actually is. I can't look at her anymore.

"You can stay out here until Lenny comes and gets you, but remember, Ouch in the car and at the new house..."

"But never, ever at the hospital!" she finishes for me.

"That's right. You got it."

"High five!" she shouts, and Hamilton and I both lean down to give her a high five. "Another one, Hambone!"

Hamilton gives her palm another slap.

"Another one!" she says, leaning toward him.

"You'll get another one after you get back from the hospital, okay?"

She sinks back down in the grass, a frown erasing her smile.

"Go," I whisper to Hamilton, and he takes one small step before I give him a shove.

"Ouch in the car and at the house," he yells over his shoulder.

"And never, ever, ever at the hospital," she replies.

We take two more steps and leave her. Now she has to do it on her own.

~

Hamilton and I are quiet as we sit side by side on the back seat of the bus.

"What do we do now?" he asks as he wipes his eye, shoving his glasses so high on his nose they crunch against his eyebrows. I want to say I don't know, because that's the truth.

"Think of a plan, I guess." I lean my head against

the scratchy fabric-covered seat. "I'll stop by Crossroads tomorrow to make sure it worked…."

"What if it doesn't?"

"Don't worry about that until it happens. I'll check on her tomorrow to make sure everything turned out okay. Then we can make a new plan. A bigger plan. The final plan."

Hamilton leans back beside me, his shoulder pressed against mine.

"Our plan didn't work last time."

I shake my head. "This isn't the same type of plan. This one isn't to get her a new home. It's just to keep her out of the bad one for a couple more days."

"I'm starting to think my greatest accomplishment of seventh grade is going to be lying more times in one year than I have in my whole life." Hamilton rubs the dark black edges of his eyes, smearing the makeup toward his temples.

"Don't look at it that way. You're telling a good lie. And you did a great job with Meridee. You're a good teacher. Maybe your biggest accomplishment this year will be saving someone's life."

"As long as they don't take out her appendix."

"As long as she stops playing Ouch."

"Ouch in the car. Never, ever at the hospital."

We both groan, folding our arms over our stomachs and the appendixes safe inside them.

~

My cheek is cool against the desk in Marjorie's office, and I close my eyes, hoping my pounding headache will go away. I could go downstairs and have Marjorie make me a cup of tea with too much honey, give me a cool towel for my forehead, but I know it won't help. I'm not sick. I feel awful about telling Meridee she might live with her mom again. I don't know if her mom will ever come back. Some do. A lot don't.

I stare down at the assignment I'm supposed to be writing for Mr. Ramirez, an essay about farming techniques in early Texas. Marjorie gave me extra computer time tonight, and normally I would race to finish it so I could use the computer to work on my business—research families, update my questionnaires—but tonight I don't even care to get started. All my brain power is focused on Meridee, a little alarm constantly ringing: Meridee! Meridee! Meridee! I look down at the prompt again and type it into Google. I don't bother to use the proper search terms Mr. Ramirez taught us last week and get flooded with over forty thousand responses. Who cares about farming in early Texas? Who cares about farming now?

I open a website, starting to read the thousands of words on the page. My head throbs. I can't do this right now....

Yes. I can. I go back to the search entries and scroll back several pages. I find an article on the Missouri River College website. Mr. Ramirez would hate that I'm using information from 2002 ("Too old! You guys weren't even born yet!"), but he'd be even more upset by what I do next.

I copy several paragraphs and paste them into a Word document. I make sure to write a topic sentence with the opening phrase Mr. Ramirez likes and swap out a few words that are too big, even for me. I add the required "Why this topic is important" conclusion, even though it isn't important at all. I change the font and add my name at the top. I know it's wrong, that it's cheating, but today I don't care. I have always done my best work in his class, so this one mistake won't matter. I always do my best at everything, but that doesn't change anything, doesn't make things okay. Today, I'm going to use my energy to save Meridee.

I hit PRINT and drop my face back to the desk.

I'm a cheater, but maybe I'm more of a Robin Hood. Sometimes you have to do wrong to get what's right.

# NIGHTMARES

I haven't had a nightmare in a long time. Years, probably. But last night, I could feel it coming before I even fell asleep. The room seemed darker when Marjorie closed the door, the blowing branches outside creating shadows on the floor, their movement a menacing dance, daring me to close my eyes and let the memories come. I tried to pull the covers tight, tucking them along the edges of my body the way I did when I was a kid, hoping that I could make myself untouchable as long as no one could pull the sheets out from around me. Each time my eyes blinked, I saw a car door opening and me stepping out onto the moonlit sidewalk, making my way behind the red-haired caseworker as we trudged up the creaking wooden stairs. I could stop my thoughts before the dream door opened, but only until I fell asleep.

Then I heard them. The dogs.

All night long.

The whimpering of their cries, the flashing of their bared teeth. I can't shake their barking from my head.

~

The fluorescent cafeteria lights flicker, and I stifle a yawn, hoping I can make it through tutoring without falling asleep. It's only one missing assignment plus a low quiz score, but our math teacher Ms. Hulsman is a real stickler about grades. I look down at the neon-yellow sticky note attached to the math quiz in my hand. "Please redo because…" I scan the five potential boxes that could be checked. I have two. One for "Lacks Mastery of Key Concept," which should really be a "Lacks Effort," because it's not that I don't know how to calculate slope, I just didn't prioritize it over saving a life. The second is "Sloppy Handwriting," which seems harsh because my handwriting is fine, and I was only putting dots on a map. How could I mess that up?

Now I can't go to Crossroads to check on Meridee. All day I've imagined different scenarios, trying to focus on the happy ones, which include her watching cartoons and eating cups of red Jell-O on the hospital bed. I hope Meridee's there or back at Crossroads, nestled among her Barbie parts.

Across the tutoring table, Hamilton stares at his identical sticky note while Piper texts on her phone. Marjorie is going to flip. Especially because of the "Sloppy Handwriting." I hope Hamilton didn't get one. She's fine with "Lacks Mastery of Key Concept," because that "just means more learning needs to be done," but she can't stand "Lacks Effort" or anything regarding penmanship. I think she taught Hamilton to print before he could walk.

"We have to shoot the next installment tonight, so you better fix that quiz quickly," Piper tells Hamilton. "How many questions did you even get wrong?"

"Six," Hamilton says. "But she's going to make me redo it all."

"Six!" Piper cries.

He nods. "Plus, 'Sloppy Handwriting' and 'Lacks Effort.'"

That's worse than I expected. That level of sticky note is almost unrecoverable. "Sorry," I say, patting his shoulder.

He shakes his head and peels the plastic layer off

the top of his snack packet, pulling out the mini Red Delicious apple. He rubs it on his sleeve like a street urchin in a novel before taking a bite.

"How long will it take to fix?" Piper asks.

"Not long," Hamilton says, his eyes focused on the quiz. He bites his lower lip as he mutters corrections to himself.

"Great, because my mom is going to be here at four fifteen to pick us up and take us to Target to get some more brushes and fishnet tights."

"You can't go," I tell Hamilton. "Ms. Hulsman already e-mailed your mom."

Hamilton drops his head into his hands. "Yard work."

"But we have to shoot tonight!" Piper cries. "Or we'll lose momentum!"

"Sorry, Pipe." He turns to me. "What about…you know?"

"I need to call and at least check on her," I whisper to Hamilton, Piper temporarily distracted, her fingers flying as she sends a text. "Make sure they didn't…" I make a slicing gesture at my stomach. "But there's no way we have phone privileges until next week. I don't think we can risk another classroom phone break-in."

"No way," Hamilton says before groaning. "Stupid 'Lacks Effort.'"

"Stupid 'Sloppy Handwriting.'"

"So, you failed, too?" Piper asks before grabbing Hamilton's bag of sunflower seeds and tearing it open with her teeth.

"I didn't fail. I just didn't meet my academic potential." Thanks, Ms. Hulsman, for the perfect comeback.

"Aren't you just so proud to know Hamilton, especially now that he's getting famous? It must be great to have such a cool family member, since your real family is…you know…" She pops a handful of sunflower seeds into her mouth.

"My real family is what, Piper?"

Her face blushes a cherry red. "You know, they're just…" She hikes her shoulders up to her ears.

"Just what? I didn't know you met them."

"I just meant that you're lucky to have such nice people to live with, since you don't have anyone else."

"Good thing I only need me."

I turn in my seat, distracting myself with my own bag of sunflower seeds when I spot an unexpected face: Lenny. He's chatting with the after-school monitor. I've never seen him outside the shelter. Did he come to tell me in person that Meridee is hurt? Did something go horribly wrong in the middle of her totally unnecessary appendectomy?

Maybe. Or…

He makes eye contact with me from across the room.

He knows.

He waves to the woman who is now helping a student fill out his club form. Lenny whistles as he walks, his muscular arms swinging back and forth.

"Hello there, Ms. Sharma," Lenny says, towering above me. "Staying after school?"

"Yep. Math tutoring."

"Glad to see you're keeping busy."

He's so calm it's freaking me out. Maybe it's fine. Maybe he doesn't suspect anything.

"Aren't you Pavi's foster brother?" Lenny asks, leaning across the table to shake Hamilton's hand. His huge hand swallows up Hamilton's tiny one, like thunderclouds enveloping the moon. "I didn't get to really meet you last night. You two rushed off to some…activity."

I gulp. Hamilton darts a frightened look at me. *Be cool.*

Lenny turns his attention back to me. "Can we talk for a minute, Pav?"

"My teacher will be here to pick us up for tutoring in a minute. It's almost three forty-five."

"No problem. I'll be quick. Let's go sit on the benches. It's a nice day out."

Outside, the breeze on my cheeks gives me a moment of hope, but Lenny's silence makes me nervous again. He finally takes a seat on a picnic table in the center of the courtyard. He rests his hands on the scuffed tabletop.

"Pavi."

I don't say anything, but do my best to maintain eye contact. It's his eyes that calmed me when I checked into Crossroads two years ago, when all I had was desperation and a plastic bag full of clothes. They're the soft eyes that once allowed me to share about my mom, the same ones that reprimanded me when I stole from other kids (I did that for a while—bad habit, I know; I stopped). Those eyes oozed empathy when I talked about teachers making me write Mother's Day cards, eyes with so much understanding, he had to have grown up in the system, too. His eyes make me want to tell the truth, they always have, but I can't. Not this time.

When I don't take the bait, he continues. "Something weird happened last night with Meridee. I wanted to ask you a few questions, since I know you visited her."

"Yeah, sure," I say, trying to keep the words "Is she okay?" from screaming out of my lips.

Lenny rubs a hand against his chin.

"Did she seem sick when you saw her yesterday? Maybe she was complaining about her stomach or her head?"

"No," I say, shaking my head slightly. "But I did…"

Lenny takes a quick breath; he thinks I'm going to confess.

"I did give her some candy. A lot of candy. Tootsie Rolls. Mini Snickers. Oh, and a lollipop. I'm really sorry. I know little kids shouldn't have sweets, but I knew she was going to a new home and I felt bad. Did she get sick? Did she throw up? I didn't think it was that much.…"

"Hey, hey, calm down," Lenny says, his eyes squinting at me like he doesn't believe my apology. "She's fine.…"

Thank goodness. I've been waiting for him to say that.

"But her caseworker said she acted really strange when she was in the car on the way to her placement, moaning and groaning, and it got so bad they took her to the emergency room, but once she got there she was fine."

She did it! Sick in the car, but not at the hospital!

"Maybe she was nervous?" I suggest.

"I thought so, but apparently she said, 'Did I do a good job at Ouch? Can I see Mama now?'"

The blood drains from my face.

"It seems she was playing some sort of game, Ouch, and…" He turns to stare straight into me. "I was wondering what you knew about that."

*Breathe, Pavi*, I tell myself. *You haven't lost yet. You just need to think. Meridee is fine, so now save yourself. And Hamilton.* A partial lie here is better than a full lie. He won't believe me without a hint of truth.

"Ouch is a game we played. I'd pretend to be sick and then she'd heal me with that old doctor's cart? By the play kitchen? You know the one with the little stethoscope and the plastic hammer? It doesn't have the mask anymore. She's interested in science, and you know most girls drop out of STEM courses by middle school because they don't think they're good at math or science, so I thought this would be a great game." I sound like Hamilton. "I've been playing Ouch and letting her heal me, but I never thought she'd do it for real."

Lenny stares at me. "Why would she think playing the game would get her to her mom?"

"Because…" I drop my head, knowing the truth I'm about to tell will rip a hole through any trust I have with Lenny. "I told her if she did her best at Crossroads she would get to see her mom. I didn't mean about the game!"

"You know you can't tell a kid that! Her being good

isn't going to get her to see her mom. Her mom is the one who needs to do right."

"I know, it was stupid," I say, because I do know. I know it doesn't matter how good your grades are, or how much the foster family likes you. You can't bring your parents back. I know that. But now Lenny won't trust me with the new kids anymore.

"I forget sometimes that you're still a kid, Pav, and you aren't always going to say the right thing. Thankfully, they just gave her some juice, and her caseworker was able to take her to her placement."

"What? She didn't go back to Crossroads?"

"No. She wasn't sick, so they took her to her family. I know you have bad feelings about them, but everything was fine."

Suddenly the sound of dogs begins to fill my brain, dragging me down, and everything starts to get heavy around the edges. My brain zooms through the images: her pink shoes stepping down onto the cracked sidewalk, the creak of the wood as she climbs the stairs, the barking of the dogs that will fill her nightmares. He has no idea what's waiting for her there.

"Pavi, are you okay?"

Lenny leans toward me, and suddenly I am up and running toward the school.

"I have to get to tutoring. I'm already late."

"Pavi," Lenny yells, but I slide into the main building behind the last kid headed to tutoring. Once inside, I crouch down in the center of the stairwell, tears beginning to fall to the beat of my pounding heart.

She's there. We didn't keep her out.

# AT LEAST HER ORGANS
# ARE SAFE

At the sound of slow footsteps on the stairs, I hold my breath, not wanting the person to know I'm crying. I keep my head in my hands, knowing instantly it's not a teacher, since they would have asked me already if I'm okay. I'm hoping the kid will pass, but the footsteps stop next to me and I can feel a presence hovering over me.

"I'm not a monkey in a zoo, so move on du—" I look up to see Santos staring down at me. He has a new hoodie, a navy blue one, and his white earbuds dangle beside the white cords, the boom of heavy bass streaming from his headphones. He's holding a folded piece of paper while he watches me.

"What? Stop staring." I get up from my crouched position and run a finger underneath my damp eyes. He watches me without a word. "You're not going to say anything?"

"Nothing I say is gonna make it better."

"You don't even know what's going on."

He shrugs. "Am I wrong?"

No. He's not, unless he's about to reveal that his earbuds are really a time travel machine that can transport me to the Nickersons' so I can pull Meridee back out the front door.

"What are you doing here, anyway? There's no way you're here for tutoring."

He unfolds the paper in his hand and holds it toward me. It's a permission slip for Music Production Club, hosted in the recording studio. "Foster lady wants me to do a club."

"Are you skipping?"

He shoves the slip back in his pocket. "Went to the wrong room. So, you gonna tell me what's wrong?"

"I guess I can. I need to get to tutoring, though."

"We can walk."

As we climb the stairs, I tell him the news about Meridee.

"At least they didn't cut her open," Santos says as we

near Ms. Hulsman's room, her classical music blaring through the door.

"She might be better off without an appendix than living where she is."

"If it's that bad, you gotta get her out."

"I know that! I wouldn't have been crying in a stairwell if everything was going to be fine."

"You're smart," Santos says. "You'll figure it out."

I take a step toward Ms. Hulsman's door. "Wait, I almost forgot: How's your foster mom?"

I can't believe I didn't ask before now. I'm never bad at my job. I'm never bad at school. Apparently, I'm only bad at saving Meridee.

"She's cool. She's Mexican, but she doesn't speak Spanish. She's been practicing with me. It's weird."

"I get that. Marjorie and Hamilton learned a bunch of phrases in Hindi when they first met me, even though I only spoke English. My mom spoke English, too." Ma sometimes called me *beti*, daughter, but mostly just Pavi-my-lovey. Sometimes other Hindi words or phrases bubble up into my head, the sounds familiar, but the meanings unclear, like having a tool I don't know how to use. Or I'll find myself humming a melody, but I won't be able to remember the words. I wonder if I'll ever want to learn more about my background. Maybe.

Right now I feel like an impostor, a fake, like I'm an actor who doesn't know their lines.

"I've gotta go," I tell Santos. "But I'll ask you more questions when we do your one-week follow-up."

He raises an eyebrow at me.

"Oh my god, I forgot, didn't I?" He nods. "What day is it?"

"Friday."

"We were supposed to meet today!"

Santos shrugs. "It's cool."

"How about Monday? Same place as before?"

"Sure," he says, popping his headphones in his ears. "Let me know if you need help with that girl." He doesn't give me a chance to respond before heading down the hall.

~

Inside the classroom, Ms. Hulsman sits behind her desk, leaning so close to her screen that she might be smudging it with the tip of her nose. Hamilton is in his regular seat, furiously scribbling. A few other kids from class are scattered around the room.

"Sign in," Ms. Hulsman snaps without looking up from her screen. Once I've filled in my information, I sit beside Hamilton, whose pencil hovers in the air as

Piper chatters away to him. She must be really bored to sit here watching him while she waits for her mom to pick her up.

"Did they?" he asks, and I shake my head.

"Is she?"

I nod.

"Man..." He sighs, banging his fist on the table. Ms. Hulsman glares before pointing up at the sign on the bulletin board, reminding us that tutoring is a RED ZONE for volume, so no talking at all unless we're working with her.

"Do you have a—" he asks, and I cut him off.

"No. Not yet."

"Oh my god, can one of you speak in a complete sentence?" Piper sighs in exasperation.

Hamilton mimics Ms. Hulsman and silently points up at the RED ZONE poster. He and I share a look, both grateful for the silence. For the moment, we have nothing to say.

# PIPER'S PLEA

**H**amilton and I are in the living room when the doorbell rings. Marjorie frowns, but we know better than to even shift in our chairs. Instead, we share a quick glance over our tattered copies of *Harry Potter*, *Half-Blood Prince* for me and *Order of the Phoenix* for him. I'm only staring at my pages tonight, not able to stop thinking about Meridee walking into the Nickersons'.

The doorbell rings again and Marjorie huffs, tossing off her quilt and setting her autobiography of Ruth Bader Ginsburg on the teetering stack of nonfiction piled high on the end table. She heaves herself out of her overstuffed chair before taking off her red reading glasses and tucking them on the edge of her shirt. Our eyes follow her to the hallway where she momentarily disappears into darkness before turning on the light.

"Piper!" she says before the creak of the door finishes.

Hamilton sets down his book, perking up in his seat. He looks over at me and I shrug my shoulders. How would I know why she's here? She's *his* best friend.

"Ms. Jennings, I know it's deep into family time, but I wanted to see if I could interrupt for a few minutes." Piper's voice is chipper, and I expect her to start a speech about raffle tickets.

Hamilton leans over the back of the couch, pushing aside the embroidered drapes.

"Her dad's parked out front," he whispers, and I picture Piper's dad texting as he waits in the SUV.

"Shh." His talking made me miss the first part of Marjorie's response. She must have invited Piper in, because we hear the front door close and Piper's voice is louder now. I wonder if she knows we are in the next room.

"To begin, I'd like to thank you for taking the time to speak with me. I've been made aware of Hamilton's declining academic performance," Piper says. "And I must say that I, too, was disappointed by this break from his potential."

"Geez," Hamilton huffs, slumping back on the couch.

"I support your decision to remove his evening outing privileges until he improves his grades, and I respect your authority as his mother to punish him as you see fit, but…"

Hamilton and I lock eyes. *But?*

"I would like to submit that while Hamilton's personal academic success has suffered in the past few weeks, the community gain from his extensive work in the online do-it-yourself (a.k.a. DIY) arena cannot be denied."

What? Is she saying what I think she's saying? I recognize the vocabulary and the argument from last year's Mock Trial competition. I didn't think Piper even liked Mock Trial, preferring creative writing, but here she is, pouring out a defense for Hamilton like the attorney general of the United States!

Piper clears her throat. "Are you aware of Hamilton's recent success with the Goth Boy tutorial on my Pretty with Piper YouTube channel?"

"I knew he made a video with you, but I wasn't aware of its…success."

Hamilton cringes.

"We currently have over one thousand views and

one hundred seventy three new subscribers to the channel. You may have even seen the flood of goth style now happening all over the school. But what you don't know is how much of an impact those videos have had on struggling youth."

"Well, then, enlighten me," Marjorie says. Piper's feet scuff back and forth between the hardwood and the welcome rug.

"Hundreds of students walk those halls feeling different, feeling weird, feeling…alone. The students who watched this tutorial might not be the star athlete or the top student. They need a role model. Dare I say a hero?" Piper clears her throat with a small cough. "Hamilton didn't just demonstrate how to properly wear black eyeliner! He gave them someone who wasn't afraid to be different!"

"Afraid to wear flour on his face," I whisper, and this time Hamilton shushes me.

"He gave them a hero," Piper says, her voice low as her feet finally stop shuffling on the floor. "And it would be a shame for them to lose their hero so soon."

There's a pause.

Is she done?

"And so, I am proposing that Hamilton be allowed to skip tonight's…in-home reflection time, and instead be allowed to join me for a fully adult-supervised filming of another YouTube video."

Hamilton is almost off the couch, his body craning to see around the corner.

"You want to film tonight?"

"Yes, so as not to…"

"Lose momentum," Hamilton whispers along with her.

"We would get all our homework done before starting production. Obviously. Hamilton can be more productive with a dedicated friend slash tutor like me."

"Thank you for being such a great advocate for Hamilton." Marjorie takes a step back to where she's almost fully visible in the doorway. "If he wants to go and completes his work, I am willing to accept your proposal."

"Yes!" Hamilton shouts with a fist pump before flying back to his spot on the couch.

"I assume you heard Piper's proposal," Marjorie says as she comes around the corner.

"Yes, ma'am." Hamilton sits up in his seat, pushing his glasses back up on his nose.

"This is a onetime trial, largely due to Piper's impressive argument, but you are still grounded for the rest of the week."

"Yes, ma'am."

Piper beams. "Dad is waiting in the car. We're going to pick up tacos on the way home."

"Okay, then. Go get your stuff."

Hamilton pops up from the couch, tucking his book onto his shelf before running out of the room, his feet flying on the stairs.

"You'll need to take Pavi with you," Marjorie says, pulling the reading glasses off her shirt. Piper turns, her lips parted in the protest I know she's forming.

"After hearing about how beneficial you'll be for Hamilton's academics, I can't let Pavi not receive similar support. I'm sure she can help with your videos, too."

"I don't know anything about makeup," I say, and Piper looks relieved.

"The studio space is really only set up for two people," Piper adds.

Marjorie gives that smile all teachers do: the one that looks nice but means "I've got all the power."

"But I'm sure we can make space," Piper says.

Hamilton trips on the last step, stumbling back into the room with an oversize duffel.

"Ready!"

"Pavi's coming, too," Piper whispers to Hamilton, and he smiles.

"Sweet!"

The three of them look over at me, and while I don't want to be involved with Piper's videos, I realize if I stay here, Marjorie will fill my evening with family-friendly activities and I won't have any time to plan. No one will care what I do at Piper's. I might even be able to use her computer for research.

"Let's do this," I say as I fold my blanket, setting my book on top.

Marjorie gives me a side hug before nudging me toward Piper. "Tell your dad I'll pick them up at eight. He doesn't need to make the drive here twice."

"Okay, Ms. Jennings. Thank you again. So. Much."

I swing my backpack over my shoulder before giving Hamilton a pat on the back.

"Let's go make you a hero."

# MERMAN

**F**rom the edge of Piper's marshmallow-like comforter, my feet don't even hit the floor. Across from me, Piper and Hamilton hover around a storage bin overflowing with craft supplies. Piper drapes a shiny blue piece of fabric over a card table before Hamilton sprinkles it with a saltshaker full of sand, pausing occasionally to sweep the sand into little dunes. Piper pulls out seashells from a large Ziploc bag, nestling them among the sand. They work methodically, as if they are saving a life and not simply making Piper feel cool.

"So, what is the theme for tonight's tutorial?" I call down from my perch, and Piper holds up a finger to me as she whisper-counts the seashells: "...six, seven, eight."

"Mer-makeup," she says as she surveys the table, a large pink conch shell in her hand.

I hop off the bed, stumbling a little from the distance. I scan the table, running my hand over the tiny shells in a Tupperware container and the pieces of fake algae.

"Don't touch anything!" Piper shouts, and I take a few steps back, leaning against the closet door.

Piper pulls out a massive makeup kit from under her bed. From the depths, she gathers an assortment of eye color palettes and brushes, and tubes of glitter and lipstick. Then comes a bedazzled jar, which looks like it used to hold baby food but now houses cotton swabs. Hamilton takes his duffel to the bathroom and returns in a bright-blue T-shirt with the seams showing.

"Your shirt's inside out," I say.

"I know, but I don't have a plain blue one. I don't think people will notice. Pipe?"

Piper turns from the brushes she's cleaning. Upon seeing him, she wrinkles her nose before rubbing on a quick swipe of gloss. She tilts her head as she assesses him.

"I thought we decided no shirt."

"I thought we decided yes shirt." Hamilton pulls at the bottom hem.

"But merpeople don't wear shirts."

"No, but I am not a merperson. I am a human being who is not going to be naked on YouTube."

"You won't be naked. You'll have pants on."

"No way."

"Don't you go swimming? You don't wear a shirt then."

"He does, actually," I say, cutting in. "Marjorie makes him. For sun protection."

Hamilton looks relieved at my support. "That's right! I always wear a shirt!"

"We might as well not even bother making the video, then," Piper says as she starts yanking the recently placed makeup containers off the table. "It won't make any sense that a merman is wearing a shirt. Besides, I wanted to do some detail work near your neck and collarbone, and I won't be able to do that if no one can see it."

Piper's eyes drill into Hamilton's, and he can't withstand the power of her stare for more than a millisecond.

"Fine. I won't wear the shirt, but can you make sure only the top of my chest is in the shot? Just my shoulders and above?"

"Of course!" She plops the makeup brushes onto the table. "Sit here."

Hamilton slinks over to the stool behind the table.

"Shirt, please," Piper says from behind the camera, and Hamilton slowly takes it off, crumpling it into a pile in his lap.

"Sit up straight," Piper chides, and Hamilton complies, but only by a few centimeters.

"We're going to start in five, four, three…" She counts two and one by holding up her fingers and then gives Hamilton a thumbs-up. Instantly his back pops rigid-straight and a commercial-star smile spreads across his face. Piper skips behind the table.

"Hello, my pretties," she says, looking straight into the camera. "Thanks for joining me today for our segment Beauty Below the Blue! Today, we'll be working with my costar, MarchingMagic612—follow him on Instagram—to demonstrate mer-makeup for all you merpeople out there."

I didn't know Hamilton had an Instagram. Marjorie will freak if she finds out.

"What's the first thing we all know about merpeople?" Piper asks into the camera.

"They're fake," I whisper, but she doesn't notice me.

Piper pauses for a few seconds like they do in kids' TV shows so the toddlers have time to answer.

"That's right! They have scales! To get this dramatic look, you'll first need to get a pair of fishnet tights. I bought these at Target, but you can get them at any store where they sell tights."

"Obviously," I mutter to myself.

Piper holds up the tights before moving toward Hamilton. It's the first time she's actually looked at him since she started filming. His frozen smile hasn't moved. "First, pull the tights over your head." While still making direct eye contact with the camera, Piper pulls the fishnets over Hamilton's head.

"Ow! My nose!" he whispers, but both of them keep smiling. She yanks a few more times before pulling them all the way under his cheek. The leg of the tights hangs from the top of his head like a really long ponytail, and suddenly I burst into laughter. Piper glares, but when I look at Hamilton's face squashed under the tights, I can't stop laughing.

"Stop! You're ruining the shot," Piper complains.

"You look like a robber!" I squeak out between laughs, my giggles almost bringing me to the floor. I don't know why I'm laughing so hard, but I can't stop.

"Pavi, stop!" Piper shouts as she walks around the table and shuts off the camera. "Now we're going to have to reshoot that part and it's going to take me longer to edit. If you can't get ahold of yourself, go outside." She points a black fingernail at the door.

"I'm fine, I'm sorry," I say between gasps. "I'm so glad I came. This is hilarious!"

"Now we need to shoot it over again!" Piper groans.

"Let me help," I say, taking a step toward the camera. "I can rewind back to wherever you want to start, and you can be ready behind the table and start right where you stopped."

"We can handle it."

"Let her help, Pipe," Hamilton counters. "We're already running late, and she knows how to work a camera."

"Fine!" Piper stomps to her place behind the table. "Let's just reshoot the whole thing, but I don't have a ton of space on my disk, so you'll have to delete the file first."

I inspect her old camera, most of it looking somewhat familiar from my semester in video production. I click a button that changes the focus. Wrong. Then I get the gallery of videos. I push PLAY on the first file, and Piper's voice fills the room.

"That would be manifest destiny," the Piper on the video says. She's sitting behind a table that is dressed like a school desk: papers, folders, a container of pencils and highlighters. "Wow, Piper, you're so quick to answer," she continues in a different voice I assume is supposed to be a teacher. "Do you have any other intelligent thoughts to add to your peers' knowledge?"

"Turn that off!" Piper says, her cheeks flaming.

"What is this?"

Piper's video voice explains the benefits of manifest destiny in language I'm sure she memorized from the textbook.

"It's nothing. Turn it off."

"Did you…video yourself practicing for school?"

"That's my private stuff!" Piper rounds the table as I start laughing again. Now video Piper is writing things on a blank piece of notebook paper, occasionally reaching a hand up to push back her blonde strands of hair.

"Hamilton, come see this!" I begin to giggle again, and Piper reaches for the camera.

"That is PRIVATE!" she shouts as she attempts to turn it off.

"Give it to her, Pavi," Hamilton says from his perch on set.

"I swear to god if you break this camera…"

"Fine," I say as I step back. "It's all yours."

"You were not supposed to see that," she says, quickly turning off the camera, her face brighter than her candy-apple lip gloss.

"Obviously! Who records themselves practicing for school? Do you watch this and take notes?"

"No! Well, yes, I watch it, but I don't take notes."

"I think it's fine," Hamilton says. "A lot of professional speakers tape themselves. It's a great way to practice."

"Those people are professionals!"

"Enough, Pavi." Hamilton's tone stops me, and I don't look at him for the disappointment I know I'll see on his face. I don't know what I'm doing. I just can't with Piper right now, and her perfect life and her tiny problems.

"Why don't you just go?" Piper says as she busies herself with the table props. "You're only here because you don't have any friends of your own. It must be embarrassing: don't have your own family, don't have your own friends."

"Piper!" Hamilton gasps, putting a hand on her arm. "That is not okay! Pavi does have a family, and it's me."

The room is quiet as I walk toward the door. It's not the first time someone has said this to me, looking at me with pity or disgust because they think my family left me. That they didn't want me. They don't know how strong you have to be to make it on your own.

"I know you need your followers and your teachers

and everyone around you to tell you you're perfect, Piper, but I don't." I grab my backpack from the floor. "I'll go wait downstairs."

"Wait, Pav…," Hamilton starts to say, but I close the door before he finishes.

Downstairs, I tell Piper's dad that I'm going to do homework in the kitchen, where it's quiet, but really, I just stare at my science worksheet. There's a pit in my stomach as I think about Piper's secret video; she was so desperate to look confident and smart, and to be honest, I don't blame her. I mean, my whole business is based on helping foster kids be perfect so they'll be safe and happy with their new families. I even have kids practice their Front Door Face in the mirror. We all have parts of our lives we're embarrassed about, things we want to hide. Most people just aren't caught on video.

Then it hits me. I know how to save Meridee.

# THE NEW PLAN

Sitting in the back of Marjorie's station wagon, Hamilton and I are grateful that her singing is filling up the car. At first he was still mad about what happened at Piper's house, but once I said "Meridee," all irritation disappeared. So now, as Marjorie belts out the chorus of her favorite Aretha Franklin song, Hamilton and I converge over the center seat and I whisper my brilliant new plan.

"Hidden cameras? Like, set up in their house?" Hamilton moves the seat belt so it doesn't cut into the side of his neck.

"Sort of, but we don't need to set them up. We'll just show up, film, and get out."

"Do we need night vision? I don't know if that's a camera or a program. I could look!"

"Shh…," I whisper as Marjorie's eyes dart back at us in the rearview mirror. I flash my best we're-just-reviewing-homework smile, and she winks before her bright-red lips burst open with a booming low note.

"We just need a camera." I look him straight in the eyes, knowing my request will take some convincing. "Piper's camera."

Hamilton's eyes grow as his head begins to shake. "No way. Cammie is her most prized possession."

"Cammie?" I say, rolling my eyes. "You've got to be kidding."

"First it was Camilla Cameron, but that's really hard to say in the middle of a shoot."

"Whatever. She won't let me borrow it, but she'll definitely let *you* have it."

He pulls out his notebook, turning to a blank page and writing "New Plan" and the date at the top. He puts "Get camera" next to number one, with a subbullet listing all the potential camera options: Piper (with a frowny face), library, and friend of Mom's.

"How are you two not grooving back there?" Marjorie asks, a bit breathless.

"We don't groove, Mom."

Marjorie smiles, pointing one finger up as she begins a classic disco move. "I thought you kids liked old-school stuff. Vintage." She switches into a new dance move, this one improvisational, her arms swirling across the front seats in a wave.

"This isn't vintage," Hamilton says. "It's just old."

"An oldie but a goodie," Marjorie argues, turning the volume up higher and beginning to sing along. We give her a little shimmy before diving back into the conversation.

"I'll check at school on Monday," Hamilton says, "but I need to know exactly what we are filming. Otherwise I won't know what equipment we need."

I pause. He's right. He needs to know, but I'm not sure I'm ready to say it. I must be lost in thought, because suddenly Hamilton's hangnail-infested fingers are snapping in front of my face. "Pavi!"

"Fine.... We need to get the...dogs in action, and potentially the people, too."

"Okay...," Hamilton says, adding "Dogs?" and "People?" to his notebook. "And the dogs we will be filming are going to be...doing what?"

"They'll probably be in their cages, but if we go almost any night around eight, we might be able to catch them...fighting."

Hamilton's nose crinkles. "Dogfighting? Like…" He waves his hands around, looking for the words to describe something I bet he can't even imagine.

"Yes…like that."

"Is that why…," he begins to ask, and I nod, knowing exactly what he's going to say.

Is that why I freaked out at his birthday party last year? Why I panicked when his neighbor's boxer with slobbery jowls leaped toward the birthday cake I was sitting beside, his eyes bulging as he flew through the air? I was certain his open jaws were for me.

I screamed.

So loud that Marjorie did, too, her voice an echo of my pain, and soon people were running and the dog was darting under the table and suddenly I was in the center of a circle of strangers, their eyes wide as they watched me cry.

That ended the party, the rest of the parents gathering up their kids, whispering theories about my childhood. "Foster kid," they mouthed to each other, their lips pursing as they shook their heads in pity. They didn't know. No one does.

I didn't tell Marjorie why I panicked. She didn't force me; she and Hamilton just crouched beside me, her hand on my shoulder, his hand on my knee.

Back in the car, Hamilton pats my hand as we pull up to our house. "It's okay, Pav. We'll figure it out."

He writes "dogs" next to number two on his list. This time it's in all caps.

~

Lying in bed, I press my nose and my toes to the wall, leaving an ocean of space in the sheets behind me. I still sleep like this, crammed close to the wall, even though Ma doesn't need the space to lie down, her hair smelling like the grease from the fryers, but also like home. I don't know how long I've been lying here, unable to fall asleep. I tried to go over the plan for Monday, making a checklist of all the things we need to do, but my thoughts keep being interrupted by a memory. It's fuzzy, like most of my memories are, but I can see myself sitting on the closed toilet seat in the dark bathroom while Ma created shadow puppets behind the shower curtain. There's no sound in my memory, her voice on mute, but I can see her delicate hands moving, gliding back and forth behind the curtain like leaves creating shadows in the sunlight.

My door creaks and the memory pauses. Marjorie already checked on me when I first went to bed, but I can tell it's her by the jingle of her bracelets. I don't

190 ⚘

move, wanting her to think I'm asleep. She sits at the edge of my bed and presses a hand against my foot. I suddenly feel the need to cry, but I swallow it down. She doesn't move, and after a few minutes I let the memories come back in. With the dancing shadows and the touch of Marjorie's hand, I hope I'll be able to sleep.

## GET THE CAMERA

On Monday, I watch Hamilton from my post on the broken bleachers that line the track. It's the school's No Tardy Party, a celebration for all of us who made it to class on time the last six weeks. Hamilton is playing volleyball with Piper, waiting for the perfect opportunity to ask for her camera.

His goal is to get her in a good mood, play whatever game she wants, and once she's happy and hopefully a bit winded, he'll ask to use her camera for a birthday present for Marjorie. He'll say he wants to record several short speeches about her mom greatness combined with secret footage of her doing the best mom things. Piper loves cheesy, sentimental stuff like that. She'll want to help him plan, and he'll give her a lunch date for them to hash out the fake details, and then, tomorrow after school—it has to be then because Marjorie's birthday is Saturday and he needs time to edit—she'll hand over the camera.

Hamilton's clearly in the get-her-happy-and-winded portion because he's eagerly jumping into the center to pass the ball, the volleyball veering wildly off his arms before he takes off running to retrieve it. I hear a loud creak behind me as someone jumps onto the back row. Santos perches like a gargoyle: hood up, earbuds in.

"Jealous?" he asks.

"What?"

"You're staring down the little dude."

"Gross. Hamilton is my brother."

He shrugs. "Not your real brother."

"He's my brother," I say, though I'm surprised by how confident I sound. I wouldn't have said he was my brother a month ago.

"How did you make it to the No Tardy Party?" I ask, certain that a guy who skips class would never have zero tardies.

"I didn't," he says, turning so his feet rest on the seat beside me. "But I have perfect attendance, so my advisory teacher let me go."

"Don't you have to attend class to get perfect attendance?"

I glance over at Hamilton, who seems to be chatting with Piper, but she is only half paying attention to him as a tiny girl I recognize from PE giggles in her other ear. Hamilton needs to bump PE girl out of the way or we're going to lose our opportunity.

Santos drops his backpack down on the seat beside him.

"Did you need something?"

He stares at me. "You said we gotta talk about my foster mom."

"We're supposed to meet after school."

"I'm here now."

"I see that," I say, looking over at Hamilton. "But I don't have my materials for your case with me." And I'm a little busy making sure Hamilton doesn't screw this up.

"Whatever," Santos says, sliding his backpack onto his back and preparing to jump down from the bleachers.

"Wait." It's not like I haven't done this appointment plenty of times before; I know all the questions by heart. I could do it with my eyes closed, or with my eyes on my weirdo foster brother. "I'll do it. Just sit down."

He remains on the bleacher above me, but does take a seat. I don't bother to ask him to take his earbuds out. Not worth it.

"Normally this session takes thirty minutes, but since things are going well at your home, it should go pretty quickly." I grab the only notebook I have with me and turn to a blank page in the back. I write his name and the date at the top of the page. "On a scale of one to ten, ten being the best possible situation and one being your life is in danger, how has your experience been in the home?"

"I don't know," Santos says, scuffing his shoe on the seat edge.

"This is just an overall preassessment. I'll get into more details later. So, overall? One to ten?"

He cocks his head to the side. "Seven."

I try to contain my surprise. I almost never get above a five, even if the family is great. Most families score low the first week. It's nothing personal; they're just new, and the kid's usually still burned out by the whole process. I don't expect an accurate score until a month in. I only ask in case it's below a three.

"Okay," I say, marking "7" on my paper. "Can you describe your sleeping situation?"

"In a bed."

"Can you add detail? Is it a permanent bed or a bed that folds out like a couch or a futon? Does the bed have a frame, or is the mattress sitting on the floor?"

"Permanent. It has wood around the edge."

"And do you have your own room?"

"Yeah."

I'm beginning to see why he scored a seven. I glance quickly over at Hamilton, who is still bumping around the volleyball.

"The next questions are all about your current diet. On a scale of one to ten, how hungry would you describe yourself at the end of an average day?"

He stares me down.

"Ten means you are stuffed, like I-should-not-have-eaten-all-of-that-I'm-gonna-lie-on-the-couch-and-turn-into-a-walrus, and one is I haven't eaten in days."

"Eight."

I write that down. "Can you describe what you've eaten so far today?"

"Are you going to ask me when I went to the bath-room, too?"

I actually do ask that question of little kids, since bed-wetting can be a sign of distress and diarrhea is an indicator of a new diet. I learned that in one of Lenny's child psychology books. I always have granola bars for those who aren't eating and a tip sheet for how to get free snacks at school. Santos doesn't need that, apparently.

"No, I don't need to know what you do in the bathroom."

"You don't need to know any of my business."

"I don't. But you asked for my help, and I can't help you if I don't know what's going on."

"I don't need help," he says, pulling down on his hood.

"Then why are you here?" I've been wasting time with him and now lost sight of Hamilton and Piper.

"I had oatmeal with this stuff on it. Berries or something. And sugar. And thick milk."

I turn to Santos. "Cream?"

He shrugs. I nod as I write down his breakfast items. "And did you eat school lunch? A or B choice?"

Suddenly a smile spreads across Santos's face.

"Your brother's coming with that YouTube girl. And she looks maaaaaad!" He bursts into laughter, rocking back in his seat as he claps his hands together.

I turn to see Piper marching toward me, her ponytail swinging, a metronome marking each stride. Hamilton is waving behind her, mouthing something I can't understand. I relax my face so I'll seem calm when she arrives.

"Hello, Pavi," she says, her hands on her hips. She looks up at Santos. "Can you give us some privacy?"

"He can be here. Just say what you need to say." Santos won't say anything, and he sort of looks like my bodyguard perched behind me with all his silent stares and smirks.

"Fine. What do you use a prime lens for?" Piper asks. Behind her, Hamilton mouths, "I'm sorry."

"What?"

"Why would you use a prime lens? For what type of shot?"

"When you need more light in your video. I took video production, too."

"Exactly!" Piper says, a maniacal grin on her face. "And when do people usually need to capture a lot of light in their film?"

I know where she's going with this, but decide to answer her questions and play innocent.

"Generally, when they're shooting in a dark location...."

"Or...," she asks, leaning toward me.

"Or?" I say, glancing at Hamilton's defeated face.

"Or at night! So why would Hamilton be using a prime lens, normally used to shoot in dark locations or at night, for a birthday video of his mom? Better yet? Why would Hamilton be asking for that lens when *he doesn't even know what it does?*"

"Sorry," Hamilton mouths again, and I shake my head at him. I'll get us out of this mess.

"He probably googled it and read the wrong information."

Piper pauses, clearly taken aback.

"Hamilton never googles wrong," she says, her confidence regained.

"Yes, I do. All the time! Last week, I…"

"Shh…," Piper and I say, and he sits on the bottom row of the bleachers.

He waves to Santos. "Hey, man."

Santos ignores him.

"Let me tell you what I think," Piper says, taking a step so close to me that I can see the glimmer in her lip gloss. "I think *you* want to shoot some film at night, maybe with your boyfriend or whatever, and you wanted Hamilton to ask me for my camera because you know he and I are best friends."

"He's not her boyfriend," Hamilton says, and Piper scoffs.

"Whatever." She turns to me. "Did you really use your own foster brother, who has taken you in when you had nowhere else to go, to get my camera for some secret troublemaking video? How could you do that to him?"

"She didn't do anything to me!" Hamilton says, popping off the bleachers. "I told her I would ask you. And it's not a troublemaking video, it is a problem-solving video, and we really need it. Really badly. So, please, Piper, can we just borrow Cammie?"

Piper's mouth opens in shock.

"Well…I…"

The school bell rings, and a crash of students begins swarming toward us, running and slinking to the tiny entrance back into the courtyard.

"Don't say no, Pipe!" Hamilton says, grabbing her shoulders. "Meet us after school and we'll talk about it. We'll tell you the truth, okay? Right, Pavi?"

I'm not thrilled, but at this point I don't have another plan. "Yeah, after school is fine. We'll talk."

"Let's go, let's go," a teacher shouts, shooing us from the bleachers.

"Hold on, everyone," I say, trying to regain control of my circus before we split for class. "Santos, meet me here after school. We'll finish your session, and you know how you said you could help? I have a job for you.

Piper and Hamilton, come here after you pick up your instruments, and we'll talk. But now, get to class. Hamilton, we canNOT get in trouble again."

The four of us step off the bleachers and into the throng of sweaty students headed toward seventh period.

# FALLING OFF THE BRINK

The class is in full cutting-and-pasting mode when Mr. Ramirez calls me to his desk. He's sitting in his rolling chair, a half-empty sticker sheet on top of the pile of essays. Everything is organized, the pencil and stapler in parallel lines, the blue to black pen ratio exact.

"Pavi," he says with an exhale. "You have always been an excellent student. Someone who always does quality work and who has creative ideas to share.…"

There's a but coming. Wait for it.

"But…" He pulls an essay from the bottom of the pile, holding it out toward me.

He knows. He knows I know he knows.

"Yes...," I say, because even though he isn't really asking a question, yes seems like the only answer.

Yes, I cheated. Yes, it's from Google. Yes, I understand I'll receive a zero and probably another punishment I didn't really think about when I did it.

"Do you know how serious this is?" he asks, and I nod. "If you were an adult you could lose your job. Or your scholarship to college."

He sets the paper down on his desk before leaning toward me. Behind me, I can feel the students nearest us cocking their heads to listen, the rhythm of their cuts and conversations slowing as they wait for his next word. The gentle piano music he has playing from his computer speakers isn't loud enough to block their snooping ears.

"I called your guardian during lunch, and she'll be here right after school. We'll meet in the front office with her and Ms. Taylor. We need to—" He's cut off by a growing roar from his electric teakettle. "Sorry. I forgot I was making tea."

He reaches over to click off the kettle, leaving the tea bag resting in his I WOOF YOU mug some kid got him for Valentine's Day. He offers me a tissue.

I refuse it, not wanting anyone to see me wipe my

eyes. They can't tell what's happening as long as my hands stay clamped at my sides.

"We need to figure out what's going on, Pavi. This isn't like you...."

We're cut off this time by the buzz of the class bell.

"We'll finish this after school. I'll meet you in the front office."

Does he really think this matters? A stupid essay about farming techniques that I will never need to know, since I have no plans to be a farmer? Do the grades of a seventh-grade kid matter to anyone but parents? I don't have those. Know what does matter? Real life. Real people like Meridee. And if I had to do it over again to help her, I would.

~

After school, I fly down the hill to the bleachers to where Santos, Piper, and Hamilton are already waiting.

"Oh good, you're here," Hamilton says when I reach them. "I was just telling Piper about Meridee."

"What about Meridee?"

Hamilton recoils at my tone, sliding his glasses up his nose with his pointer finger.

"Just that you met her at Crossroads, your old shelter,

and that she is living with one of your old foster families and how we don't want that."

I breathe. Okay. That wasn't that bad.

Santos pulls a single Hot Cheeto out of his hoodie pocket, and I almost lunge for it, suddenly craving the tang and spice.

"I thought you could explain what we need the camera for," Hamilton says, setting me up to take over the conversation before he steps to the edge of the grass. I put a hand over my eyes to block the bright afternoon sun.

"We need to get some film evidence of the family that we can use to help persuade Meridee's caseworker to send her somewhere else."

"What type of evidence?" Piper asks, the back of her swinging tennis shoes clanging against the bleachers.

"Just some...events, okay?"

"They're a bad family, Pipe, trust me," Hamilton adds, and she shakes her head.

"I'm all for helping a little girl, but I'm not going to some criminals' house without you telling me what's going on. How bad are they? Are we talking robberies? Or human trafficking? We learned about that in World Cultures last year, and it is really a problem."

"They're bad enough. That's all you need to know." I take a step so that I'm one inch closer to her than is comfortable. Even though I'm below her, I don't break eye contact. "You don't have to help us. I didn't even want to ask you, but Hamilton said you were the best person for the job."

Her face twitches; I have her hooked. Only took a compliment.

"Okay, god, I'll loan you the camera; I just wanted to know what was going on."

"You'll know what you need to know," I say, checking to see if Santos is listening. It's then I notice he doesn't have his earbuds in; they're drooped around his neck, the white ends dangling beside the ties of his hoodie. He looks up, staring straight into my eyes, and I answer the question he's silently asking.

"Really bad."

"How?"

I instantly think in terms of foster care urban legends, the stories that swirl around the shelters and playgrounds, some nightmares, some daydreams.

"Not the cannibal family, but not the just-ignore-you bad."

His lips tighten as he digests that information, his brain surely jumping to the visions of a family sitting down to a dinner of their latest foster kid. We all knew that there's no way a foster kid could actually get served for dinner. No one could get eaten, at least not in that sense. We get consumed all the time, but not with forks and knives.

"What does that mean?" Piper asks. "Why does he get to know?"

"It's a foster kid thing."

Piper huffs. "So when are you planning to shoot this?"

"Tonight."

"What?" Hamilton asks, taking a step toward me. He leans in and whispers, "We don't have a plan yet for tonight. I need some time to develop logistics and—"

"We need to film it tonight." I don't know how long I will be grounded, and it's not like I can get in much more trouble anyway.

"I have ballet after school on Monday nights," Piper says.

"You can go to ballet, just see if you can drop off the camera at our house on the way. Say Hamilton needs it for a project."

"You're not getting my camera without me. I'll cancel ballet." She claps her hands and turns to Hamilton. "Now we can shoot another video! Before we film Pavi's thing!"

"We need your camera. We don't need you," I say.

"Excuse me?"

"She should come," Hamilton says, reaching out to place a hand on my arm. "It is her camera, and we could use the help."

"We don't need another person to possibly get caught."

"Why's he here, then?" Piper asks, her thumb pointed at Santos. "What's he offering?"

"He's going to do surveillance." I turn to him. "I'll explain in a minute."

"It's me and the camera or no camera," Piper says, raising her eyebrows in challenge. "You said you couldn't do it without me...." Ugh. I need her and she knows it.

"Fine, but this is not going to be like one of your DIY videos. I'm in charge. My plan. My rules. You bring the camera and stay out of the way."

The school's call system crackles over the field.

"Pavi Sharma, please report to the front office immediately. Pavi Sharma to the front office."

Hamilton's head whips to me.

"Why do you have to go to the—"

"I'll tell you later. No time now. The plan…"

I look at all three of them, and I hope they're ready to do this. I hope it's something we can even do.

"Santos, do you remember the address from the phone call? It's 702 Lovely Lane. Do you think you could skip your after-school club and go there? We need to scout out the house again, check for nosy neighbors, broken glass in the backyard, anything dangerous since we'll be there at night. I can pay you back for your bus ride."

"I got it," he says, pulling on his hoodie cord.

"Tonight, we all meet here by the lamppost at eight. Can everybody sneak out?"

"Definitely. I've done it before," Piper says, her hands on her hips.

I doubt she really has, but maybe her confidence will help Hamilton, who is starting to hyperventilate.

"Okay, then. We'll meet here and then take the bus to the Nickersons'. Do NOT tell anyone where we are going. Dress in black. Comfortable shoes. Be here at eight. I gotta run."

I leave them on the field and take off running back toward the school. I feel myself starting to be pulled under, but I just have to keep my head above water long enough to reach Meridee.

I slow down when I get to the sidewalk outside the main office. Through the front window, I see Marjorie laughing with the attendance secretary, her hand on the woman's shoulder as the two of them shake. Mr. Ramirez leans against the back wall, furiously texting with one hand as he adjusts his red bow tie with the other. A few parents are sitting in the chairs across from the front counter, and I take a deep breath before grabbing the metal handle and yanking the door open.

The tone of the room changes as Marjorie spots me, disappointment filling her eyes. Suddenly Ms. Taylor comes out of her office, adjusting her earpiece as she waves toward us. "So sorry to keep you all waiting. So many phone calls! Come in! Come in!"

She ushers the three of us into her office, and Marjorie and Mr. Ramirez pause at the door to introduce themselves and shake hands. Ms. Taylor pulls three chairs into a semicircle around her desk before patting the center chair.

"This is for you, Ms. Sharma."

I take a seat, resting my backpack on the floor as Mr. Ramirez and Marjorie sandwich me. Ms. Taylor reaches down to rub her ankle and I think I hear her shoe clunk to the floor. If I smell body odor in a few minutes, I'll know she took it off. She straightens a folder on her desk before adjusting the earpiece of her radio again. "It seems we need to talk, don't we, Pavi?"

She stares at me, her eyelashes so long they seem to close in slow motion each time she blinks. I count three eyelash flaps before she says something. "Do you have something you need to tell us?"

"Didn't Mr. Ramirez already tell you what happened?"

"We do in fact know the details," Ms. Taylor says, "but we want to give you a chance to tell your side. We are here for *you*."

"What's going on, Pavi?" Marjorie asks, reaching out a hand to place it on my knee. Her nails are painted. Red. She must have done that last night after we went to bed. I notice the thumb even has a little flower painted on it. She always offers to do mine. I've never said yes.

When I don't say something right away, Mr. Ramirez jumps in. "I'm really surprised by this downturn. First with breaking into my room…"

Technically it was unlocked.

"And now with the plagiarism? You're so smart, Pavi. I don't understand why you would need to copy someone else's work."

I wish I had my full brainpower to think. What explanation will get me in the least amount of trouble? I could say something about the pressure of the magnet program. I know the counselor has a lunch bunch for all the stressed-out kids.

"Is it that boy?" Marjorie asks, her hand now on my shoulder.

Thank you, Marjorie, for the perfect excuse!

"Yes..."

"I appreciate you being honest with us," Marjorie says before Ms. Taylor jumps in.

"Yes, thank you, Pavi. So, is he telling you to do these bad things? You know, he's..."

"I'm not concerned about the boy," Marjorie says. "I'm concerned about you, Pavi."

"I'm a little unclear how Santos resulted in you copying your Texas history essay," Mr. Ramirez says, his head tilted as he looks at me. "The eighth graders have US history, so there's no connection between the classes."

Thankfully, I do have a true answer for this one, if I mix the parts of my life in the right combination.

"He moved to a new foster home." True. "And I wanted to spend time with him before he left, since I won't get to see him much anymore." True-ish. "We got to talking about his new foster family and then I forgot about the essay, and I didn't have time to write it the next day." Half true. "I know I made bad choices, and I should have asked for an extension, but I'm so worried about not doing well in the magnet program. I don't really fit in here, and Santos gets me. He knows what it's like, and I don't feel so different around him."

I realize as I'm talking that it's actually true. As

much as I like hanging around Hamilton, there is something different when I'm with Santos. It's like we're novels in the same series; I don't have to give him a synopsis of my pages because his are the same. Different characters, different setting, but the same themes. I don't have to hide the scary parts of my life because chances are he's lived them, too.

"Oh, Pavi," Marjorie says, her red-tipped fingers curling around mine. "I know it's hard, and I haven't done a very good job of asking how you're really doing. You always seem so in control!"

I turn to Mr. Ramirez. "Can I write the essay again? You don't have to give me full credit or anything." I really do want to do better. Not that I can write it tonight, but I want to be his top student again.

"That sounds like a good plan."

All I have right now are plans. Plans to save Meridee. Faulty plans like faking appendicitis, and hopeful plans to film the Nickersons.

Right now, I need my plans to start becoming my reality.

# SOLIDARITY

"Ugh, my knees," Hamilton moans from across the backyard path. Beneath his legs are his sweatshirt and a folded lawn bag, but apparently this combination isn't doing enough to protect his joints while we weed. "I'm going to need a knee replacement when I'm old. I can feel it already."

"You don't have to do this," I say as I work my screwdriver under the root of a large dandelion. "Get ready to go to Piper's. You're not the one who's grounded."

"I stand...kneel...in solidarity with you for this unjust punishment."

"Your mom's not out here; you don't need to give a speech."

Hamilton scoots forward on his paper bag to toss a weed into the orange bucket on the path between us.

"I thought parents weren't supposed to do this kind of punishment anymore."

"It's not punishment," I say as I dig my screwdriver deeper into the ground, enjoying the pressure and flying dirt. "It's 'an opportunity to reflect on my choices.' Don't you pay attention to your mom at all when she talks about school?"

"We are not her students."

I creep an inch forward on my own folded lawn bag toward a small collection of weeds lining Marjorie's flower bed. "It's not that bad out here."

I actually appreciate being trapped, to not be able to do anything but dig and toss, dig and toss. It's like my brain has been forced to relax, something I need before we head to the Nickersons' tonight. I try to block out the memories, but with each second that moves us closer toward that door, I can hear the barking, the sounds filling my head and unbalancing the rhythm of my heart.

I'm going back.

"Have you ever done this before?" Hamilton asks, stretching his arms behind him. "Rescue a kid like this?"

"No, I've never needed to."

"So, most times things aren't this bad?"

For a moment, when I look at his freckled face and the way his glasses are crooked on his nose, I think about lying to him. I don't.

"Sometimes they're worse. But I couldn't fix those. This one I can help."

Hamilton nods before turning back to the weeds. We're quiet as we crawl across the ground, the only sounds the thud of a weed landing in the bucket and the faint notes of Marjorie's jazz music coming from the open kitchen window.

"Who got you out?" Hamilton asks.

"What?"

"You used to live at the Nickersons'. We're rescuing Meridee, but who rescued you?"

I didn't get rescued.

"I was only a short-term placement. Eight months. My mom was in court, so when it ended I went back to her for a little while."

She tried really hard that first time. Went to all the classes, showed up on time to all the visitations. When she'd reach her arms out to me and I'd fold into them, she didn't smell like cigarettes or spoiled milk, but like our laundry detergent, the powder kind in the orange-and-yellow box. When she clasped her hands around my face, I knew she was really seeing me. I never told her what was going on at the Nickersons'. She was trying so hard to feel better, and I didn't want to ruin anything. If she could fight for me, then I could hold on as long as she needed. I was so relieved the day I finally left that house. I didn't know that I would be a stranger in another person's home again. I didn't know that my mom would eventually stop showing up.

Hamilton stops and sits on his paper square. "What's your mom's name?"

"Why?"

"Just wondering."

"Meera." Her name falls from my mouth. I haven't said it in years, haven't said it that many times in my life, actually. When I lived with her I called her Ma, but I've been gone so long that I haven't had the chance to say her real name. Meera.

There's a pause as Hamilton half-heartedly scratches in the ground. I wait for the question he wants to ask.

"When is the last time you saw her?"

"I don't know."

"You don't remember?"

"I don't remember."

He wants to argue with my memory, but I stare at him and he bites his lower lip before reaching to push up his glasses.

"Okay…," he whispers, his eyes dropping to the dandelion below him, his breath heavy as he tugs.

# 26

## THE CREW TAKES ON THE NICKERSONS

Standing under the lamppost at the far end of the football field, I scan the dark edges beyond the glowing ring surrounding me. Hamilton and Piper should have been here five minutes ago. I pretended to be sick and then snuck out after Marjorie tucked me in bed, waiting until she started to run bathwater so the sound would cover my steps. She won't check on me again until eleven, when she goes to bed. Three hours. We'll have to be fast.

The school looks so strange in the dark, the buildings looming over the sidewalks and courtyards I pass through every day. It feels massive, ominous, overpowering me in a way it doesn't when it's full of school-day life. Finally, I spot a body moving toward me, and even though I recognize the slow walk, my heart still speeds up. Santos doesn't seem to be in a hurry, his head down, swaying side to side as he makes his way toward me.

"You made it," I say when he finally crosses into the circle of light.

"What?" he asks, pulling an earbud out from under his hood, the muffled beats sounding over the passing of nearby cars.

"Were you able to check out the neighborhood?" I ask, leaning back on the light pole, my jacket snagging on a leftover staple from the homecoming dance flyer.

"Yeah. Broken-down car across from the house. We can hide behind that. Lots of junk in the neighbor's yard, but I moved most of it so we'll have a path." He pauses, dropping his head to his shoes. "I saw the dogs. Fights?"

I nod.

"My uncle did that. Poor dogs." Santos stretches his arms above his head before dropping them by his side.

From across the field, I hear my name. Hamilton's and Piper's dark forms come running toward us. I hear both of them wheezing.

"What happened?" I yell as their forms start to take shape. A large camera bag is bouncing against

Hamilton's hip, and he keeps reaching up to keep the shoulder strap from sliding down his arm.

"I'm...so...sorry," Hamilton pants as they break out of the dark.

"We're not that late," Piper says as they slow down to a walk. Hamilton tilts to his side, pressing one hand against his diaphragm.

"We shouldn't have run. This thing gave me bruises." He drops the bag on the ground.

"We need to run again if we're going to make the bus," I say. "Wait. What's on your face?"

Two streaks of brown and green line his cheeks, and there's two swipes of black under his eyes.

"Are you wearing makeup?"

"Well...," Hamilton starts before Piper jumps in.

"I told you we were making a tutorial," Piper says, her black-gloved hands popping to her hips. "So you can't complain. You owe me, seeing as you are using my equipment. You wouldn't even have any of this production without me."

"It's not a production...."

"I don't know why you're complaining about a little tinted foundation. And isn't that our bus?" Piper tilts her head toward the stop.

We all turn to see the MetroRapid bus idling at the stoplight, only a block away.

"Let's go!" I shout, taking off toward the bus stop, Santos right behind me. I can hear the camera bag slamming against Hamilton as he huffs after us. The bus pulls up just as we are crossing the street, and I dig a Ziploc full of change out of my pocket.

"Quarters!" I hand out stacks of them, money I took from the jar Marjorie fills with coins left in our pockets before laundry.

The bright lights of the bus are jarring as we stumble up the aisle toward the empty back seats. Santos kicks his feet up onto the seat in front of him and rests his hoodied head against the glass. Once we're seated, I pull out a map of the backyard and lay it in the aisle in front of us.

"You made a map?" Hamilton asks, leaning over in his seat. "Without me? I'm great at maps. This one isn't even to scale."

We look down at the rushed pencil sketch I did on the back of an old worksheet I stole from Mr. Ramirez's recycling bin. Hamilton's right, the house is completely too small for the size of the page, and I didn't use a ruler, letting jagged lines mark out the fences, uneven rectangles for the cages. You can barely read the labels I scribbled across the different elements. I tried to slow down, to let myself remember as accurately as possible, but I couldn't spend that much time thinking about that place.

"This map is fine," I tell him as I squat down beside it. "This is the backyard, and this is the perimeter fence. This one is wood and this one is chain-link."

"The fence is all wood now," Santos adds. "Sorta tipping on the back side."

"Which way is north?" Hamilton asks. "This map doesn't have a compass rose. Or a legend. What are those dots?"

"Nothing, they're just marks I didn't bother to erase. And it doesn't need a compass rose. All you need to know is street, house, backyard." I turn the map so it's facing the rest of the troops. "This is the back door, and we should steer clear of these two bedrooms so no one hears us. If we hear any movement then we need to abort the mission."

"Which room is Meridee's?" Hamilton asks.

If it was the same as mine, then it's barely a room, more like a large closet a rich woman would have used as a walk-in. Not quite a Harry-Potter-under-the-stairs situation, but a room small enough that it barely fit a twin mattress with all the boxes lining the one wall.

"She's probably here," I say, pointing to the small

space beside the kitchen and the back door. "But we really need to focus on—"

"How we gonna get in?" Santos asks. "Pop the screen on her window? I can do that."

"Oh my god, I canNOT break into a house! I canNOT go to jail!" Piper furiously rubs another layer of lip gloss on her lips.

"We're breaking in now?" Hamilton asks. "I thought we were just filming. I should have brought better tools...."

"There's no breaking in," I say. "We aren't even going near the house."

"What? Is she going to meet us outside?" Piper asks. "In that case, can't we just call her and have her walk out?"

"We can use this," Santos says, pulling a screwdriver out of his pocket.

I look around at their confused faces. I really screwed this up.

"Who thinks we are here to kidnap Meridee?"

Santos's and Piper's hands go up while Hamilton's hand hovers by his side, half up, half down in uncertainty.

"I thought we were just filming," Hamilton says.

"But then Santos pulled out the screwdriver, and I thought maybe I didn't get the agenda change."

I sigh, running a hand through my hair before pulling my beanie back down. I can't believe I let my standards slip like this. Normally, I would have been more organized. We'd have reviewed a map I created on some free software I found online. We'd have organized supplies and several worst-case-scenario plans. All I have now is a crumpled map, some really expensive camera equipment, and three kids who apparently think we are going to commit a felony.

The bus driver announces our stop.

"Okay. Let me try again," I say as I stand, swaying for a few seconds before I grasp the bar above me. "We're going to film the dogs fighting—"

"Fighting!" Piper cries, and I hold up a hand.

"We film and then we get out. That's it. Hamilton, you be the lookout. Santos, you'll have to help me get over the fence."

We lurch forward as the bus stops and then pile down the aisle, hopping out the side door. The dark streets around us are empty, the only light the dim overhead streetlamp and the red taillights of a stalled car a few blocks away.

I adjust my jacket and shove my hands in my pockets. "Okay, let's move."

"Wait!" Hamilton whispers. "Shouldn't we do some sort of send-off? Like put our hands in the middle and say something in unison? Or maybe you could give us a speech."

"We don't have time." I step into the center of the group. We hear the first dog howl of the night. "Let's go."

# 27

## GOING BACK

My feet glide along the pavement, a half-walk, half-lunge as my body leaps over gaps in the sidewalk, my muscle memory anticipating certain cracks I can't see in the dark. I'm not afraid like I was last week when I was hoping to be wrong about the dogs. And unlike when I was nine years old and I made this two-block trip from the school bus stop alone, I don't feel sick to my stomach. The increasing nausea that used to overwhelm me is replaced by a raging adrenaline that's thumping out a beat in my veins. Behind me I hear the whispered voices of Hamilton and Piper, punctuated by far too many shushes for them to actually be stealthy, but I keep my head forward.

Somewhere behind us, I imagine Santos strolling down the sidewalk, his face invisible under his hoodie, his hands tucked into his front pocket, pulling his body forward and down the street. He blends in here, a neighborhood the rich kids at school would call sketchy, the curve of his shoulders and the pounding of his feet all a part of this rundown block no one should ever have called Lovely Lane.

At the street corner, I pause, noticing the red truck parked out front. He's home. They're home. I don't think she ever leaves. She didn't when I was there.

Without waiting for the crew, I race across the street, resting my back against the tilted wooden fence. In minutes, we are all lined up behind the fence, the only sound the scratching of the dogs' dishes against the cement, pierced by the occasional bark. A door creaks across the street and then a cacophony of barks fills the empty block, their chains clanging as they strain toward the door.

"Why are they freaking out?" Hamilton asks, turning his head to peer through the cracks of the fence.

"No more talking," I whisper, attempting to push the bile down my throat. "I'll climb over, then Piper will hand me the camera."

"It's my camera so I should be..."

I glare and she stops, the barks finally putting me in charge.

I pull my hat farther down on my head before grabbing the fence. We all work in silence now, the closeness removing any excitement and leaving us with fear. Once both my feet are on the fence, Santos steps up to place his hands on my waist, holding me steady. I wish he had been here last time I tried to do this.

"Okay, lift me on three," I whisper, prepping my toes for the push up and over the edge. "One, two, three."

Santos easily lifts my feet from the ledge, and I scramble to get both arms over the top, the wood pressing into my underarms, leaving bruises, I'm sure.

"Hold on a second." Once I confirm the backyard is empty, I give Santos the go-ahead, and he pushes me harder. I use the tiny muscles I've developed in PE and push myself over, almost falling as I swing my legs over the top, the splintered wood tearing through my leggings and scratching my ankles. I drop down into the muddy backyard, grateful for the soft landing but not the muck seeping into my shoes. My presence sends the dogs into a frenzy, and I instantly panic, nowhere to hide in the open space. I fix my loose shoe, mud covering my fingers.

"Shh, shh," I whisper, even though it won't make a difference. Nothing stops this racket.

"Shut up!" a voice yells from the house, but there is no movement at the door. I lean back against the fence, trying to stop my heart from clawing out of my chest.

"Okay, pass the camera over." Instead of the black camera bag, I find Hamilton's leg dangling over the fence.

"Get back over there!"

"Just grab my leg and pull! I'm going to fall!"

Soon his other leg is over, both swinging wildly.

"You have to stop moving or I can't grab you!"

*Crunch.* Hamilton's body drops to the muddy grass beside me.

"What are you doing? You're supposed to be the lookout," I whisper, grabbing his hand to pull him up, grateful when he doesn't wince.

"Santos can be the lookout. I didn't want you to be over here by yourself."

I frown, though his presence has caused my breathing to slow a little.

"Fine," I say before whispering through the fence toward the outline of Santos on the other side. "Pass the camera."

"Do NOT break it!" Piper loud-whispers through the fence. "Seriously, I know you guys don't get an allowance large enough to cover the cost."

"Enough!" I say, the nearness of the dogs ridding me of any patience. "Enough with your precious camera and your precious life. This is not about you! This is about a girl who needs our help, because unlike you, not everything in her life has turned out so perfect. She's just a little kid, so shut up and help us or go home."

Piper's lip trembles. "Sorry," she whispers.

That's the first time I've heard her say that.

"Can you send the camera over now?"

The fence creaks as Santos hops onto the lower ledge, reaching over the fence to hand me the small silver camera. I have to jump to grab it, careful not to slip in the mud and end up back on the ground. When the camera is secure in my hands, I turn.

It all looks the same, the metal cages filling every spare space along the back fence, the cement floors stained red and brown. A variety of padlocks hold back the frothing animals, some locks large and silver and others so small they look like they came off a kid's storybook. On the far side of the lawn is a lone dog attached by a rope to a stake in the center of a muddy field. There's also a blue barrel with an old towel inside that he must use for a kennel, and two black food dishes.

"Wow, this is a lot of dogs," Hamilton says as he takes a step toward the first cage and a large black-and-brown Rottweiler. "Hey there, buddy."

"Hamilton! Don't!"

"He's fine. He's not even really barking anymore." He leans toward the dog, his nose lining up with the foaming snout. "Hello there. What's your name?"

"That one doesn't have a name."

I gave names to the quiet ones, the ones who wouldn't snap as I poured their food through the holes in the cage. The rest got names when they fought, Killer or Giant, the same names recycled over and over again, regardless of the dog.

"These dogs look old, but otherwise they look… fine. I don't think they could fight if they wanted to," Hamilton says as he moves to the next cage. "Look at this guy, though! He's got a couple scars on his ears."

"Hamilton, get back!" I shout as he squats down beside the cage, a mere millimeter away from the gnashing teeth. "You don't know what they can do!"

"Actually, I do. I've been reading up on it. Did you know the average bite pressure of a Rottweiler tops out at about three hundred twenty-eight pounds? Isn't that crazy?"

"Deadly, not crazy."

"There appears to be no evidence of the actual fighting itself, no chairs or a ticket counter, though there are a few beer cans scattered in the mud," Hamilton says. He turns to look at me and cocks his head. "You're not even filming yet? What are you waiting for?"

I don't know, but I can't move. I can't get near them.

"Pav?" he says, moving toward where I stand with my back pressed against the fence.

"Do you guys need the bounce? For lighting?" Piper whispers.

"No, we got it," Hamilton says as he gets closer, his steps hesitant like I'm the skittish dog. "Give it to me." He stretches his hand out toward the camera. "I'll do it."

He gently removes the camera from my sweaty palms, flipping open the side screen and hitting RECORD.

"It is October twenty-second at 8:42 PM. We are here in the backyard of Mr. and Mrs. Nickerson of 702 Lovely Lane to document the violation of Section 42.10 of the Texas penal code (a.k.a. dogfighting). It appears in the backyard we have at least eight dogs, most housed in metal cages with one tied to a stake in the center of the lawn. They all appear to have food and water, though there are a few piles of dog…feces…that someone needs to scoop."

He moves toward the cages, his hand steady as he scans each one.

"Some have scars from previous injuries, most likely from the fights."

He pauses the camera and turns to me.

"This is really too many dogs for one person. And there's no way these guys can even fight. Look at them. They're super old. That one even has white whiskers."

At the sound of an ambulance a few blocks away, one of the dogs begins to howl, setting them all off again. I keep a few feet of distance as I follow Hamilton. They're all one mass of muscle and horror, until I recognize a smattering of freckles on the forehead of one white—beige from the dirt—pit bull.

"Stardust…"

"I hope they can hear me; that one is going crazy!" He points to the dog tied up to the stake, and that's when I see it. The tilt of the metal pole, the slow yielding as he lunges, the Texas ground too soft from the recent rainstorm.

"Hamilton, we need to go."

"Hold on, I need to get this last one. It has some gross cut on its leg. Pus and everything. This is perfect for the video. He probably has some sort of disease that would also make this an unhealthy environment."

He's kneels down, next to the final cage.

"Now, Hamilton!"

"Hold on," he says, the camera pressed tight to the chains.

I race across the cement toward him, sliding in some muck. I grab him by the hood of his sweatshirt.

"Look!"

The dog's body lunges an extra foot. It turns to inspect the stake, having felt the difference, the nearness to freedom.

"That's bad," Hamilton whispers before we start to run.

Our frantic energy sets the dogs howling.

"Ow!" I hear behind me, and turn to see Hamilton on the ground, the camera safely clutched above his head, blood streaming from his chin where it slammed against the cement.

"Oh my god!"

"I'm fine, just help me up!"

I grab him by his shoulders, as he still hasn't let go of the camera. We're a few feet from the fence, and I don't bother to look behind us, marking the distance of the dog only by his sound.

"Santos! Take the camera!" I grab it from Hamilton, jumping up to the top of the fence to meet Santos's waiting fingertips.

"You first," I tell Hamilton, and he doesn't argue, the loss of blood making his face white like death. "Do not pass out! You're going to be fine!"

I bend a knee and he steps up, the mud sinking through my pants, my knee aching under his weight. A drop of blood lands on my wrist as I hand his palm over to Santos. Hamilton moans as I lift his legs and then push from the bottom of his feet. There's a yelp as he lands on the other side. Santos's hands appear over the top of the fence, and I realize there is no way I can reach them without standing on something.

"Hold on!" I shout as I turn to scan the yard, not allowing myself to really look at the dog barely attached to the stake. I notice an old bucket near one of the cages and race to it, the water inside pouring down my legs as I run.

"Pavi!" Santos shouts over the barking, and I flip the bucket over and scramble atop, the plastic sagging under my weight.

"Now! Pull me up!" With one look over my shoulder, I see the dog thundering across the lawn toward me. "Now!"

Our fingers connect for a moment before the crack. His rough palms slide through my outstretched fingers, and then I am falling back to the ground.

# 28

# WAKING UP IN THE
# NICKERSONS'

My eyes open to the blue glare of a TV screen, a clammy palm stroking my forehead. I flinch and feel a sharp pain in the back of my head before realizing that it's cradled in Meridee's lap.

"It's okay," Meridee says, her voice calm as she pats my forehead, smearing sweat across my skin. "Hush, little Pavi, don't you cry. Meridee's a-sing you a lullaby."

I blink a few times, trying to get the rest of the dark room into focus, but I'm only able to decipher the light from a TV commercial for Marjorie's laundry detergent.

"Meridee, where are we?"

"We're on the bed, silly!"

Meridee bounces on the bed, jostling my head and sending another sharp pain through my skull. I reach a hand up to check the back of my head. Through my mass of hair, I feel a small bump and what might be blood but could just be sweat.

"How did I get here?"

"Poppa N brought you. He went to find a first-grade kit."

"First aid kit. Is Poppa N the man who lives here?" I know the answer has to be yes, but she can't mean Mr. Nickerson.

"Yep. His home is his camel."

"What?"

"A man's home is his camel," she says in a low voice that is a freakishly accurate representation of Mr. Nickerson.

"You mean his home is his castle?" I don't know how hard I hit my head, but nothing seems to be making sense. I try to get up and Meridee pushes my head down, her palm smashing my nose.

"Ow, Meridee, I'm fine. You have to let me get up! We have to get out of here."

I push myself up again and take in the room. It looks a lot different than when I was here. There is a desk and a small chair I don't recognize. I can't tell the wall color, but it looks a bit lighter, and I can actually see the wall without the piles of cardboard boxes. The room's bigger than I remember without them. I'm woozy when I stand up and reach a hand out, landing on Meridee's head.

"Hey! Don't bonk me!"

"Shhh. You've got to be quiet."

I press my ear to the closed door and try to listen in the hallway. No sound except for the occasional barks of dogs. "You need to wait here, okay? I'm going to…"

I don't know what I'm going to do. My head is throbbing, and I don't have a plan. We could try to sneak out the front door and make a run for it, but who knows where he's waiting. Would he try to stop us? I'm sure he was angry to find me in the backyard. Or someone in the backyard. I bet he doesn't know it's me, just some girl with a black jacket and blood on her head. And where is Hamilton and everyone else?

"Stay here," I whisper as I step into the hallway. Meridee waves before I pull the door closed behind me. My heart slams in my chest, so loud I wonder if he can hear it. The hallway is dark, and I slide along the wall, afraid to land on any creaks in the warped floor. I take a step, pause, take a step, pause. If I can figure out where he is, I can get back to the room and take Meridee out with me.

At the end of the hall, I prepare myself to look around the corner into the living room before crossing the hall into the kitchen. Maybe he's outside, checking the dogs who are still howling. With a quick inhale, I look around the corner of the living room, but it's empty. There's a throw blanket on the footrest by a cracked leather recliner, and a burnt bag of popcorn resting in the seat. The room looks almost the same as I remember, but slightly improved, as if my memories are the dusty version of the truth. It's the same couch, but the cushions look straighter. The stained lampshade has been spun to the back of the room so the dark black mark isn't showing. On a rough-cornered coffee table is a glass bowl of multicolored candies with twisted ends.

And then I spot it. On the floor in front of the TV is a small pink teddy bear. It looks new, its perfect fur a spot of joy in a familiar gloom. A gift from a heart I thought was stone. It must be Meridee's, and suddenly I can't breathe, suffocating under the weight of the past and a present I don't understand.

"You're awake," says a voice that sends shivers up my spine.

I scream as a wrinkled hand grabs my arm.

"Easy there."

I stand with my mouth agape as I look at a face that has the same wash of…hope?…that covers this house. Mr. Nickerson looks so…small. I don't remember him being this short. He has glasses now, thin wire rims that remind me of a farmer in one of the books at Crossroads. His shoulders are hunched as he extends his arm out toward me, the cuff of his plain button-down shirt sliding up to expose age spots.

"You better sit down." He watches me like I'm a startled deer as he walks toward the kitchen. "I'll get ya a glass of water."

For a second I hesitate, a moment of fight or flight or go back and get Meridee, but I follow him into the kitchen. I stand beside the fridge, the fluorescent lights above us blinding in the dark house. The dark cabinets seem crowded into this tiny room, the green countertops matching the green linoleum floor. I run my shoe along a clear piece of tape sealing a slice in the floor I used to look at every morning when I got myself a glass of water.

"I oughta call the cops on you kids," Mr. Nickerson says as he places the glass on the table, which is now covered by a faded white tablecloth and a plastic flower-basket-shaped napkin holder. "I don't know where your friends are. Musta run off." Mr. Nickerson shakes his head. "I'm not gonna call the police. I was a kid once. You lookin' at the dogs?"

"Yes," I say, my first words since the scream.

"You better sit down a minute."

He walks back to lean against the sink. I don't really want to sit down, but the throbbing in my head is making it hard to keep my eyes open. I sit on the edge of the folding chair.

"How's your head?"

"It's okay."

"Knocked you out good." He rubs a hand across the graying stubble on his chin. "Your mom better take you to the doctor, just to be sure."

"I don't have a mom," I whisper, the words pulsing out from my pain.

"Well, then, whoever takes care of you. You got someone we can call?"

I take a sip of the lukewarm water.

"Yes."

"You'll have to use the phone in the entryway. We don't have cell phones."

Suddenly Meridee's giggle pierces the silence, and Mr. Nickerson smiles. I think. It was almost too small to notice if I hadn't been staring at him.

"Goofball," he mutters. He pauses, his head cocked as he looks at my face.

"You look real familiar? Do you go to church with Janet? I don't go often...."

Janet. She leaves her room now?

"I don't go to church with Mrs. Nickerson. I lived here with you three years ago. For almost a year." Swelling inside me is a deep rage. "And for that entire time, I slept in that little room with all the boxes where you are now keeping another little girl."

Mr. Nickerson swallows, his Adam's apple bobbling in his throat.

"You're the kid who threw up on my shoe."

"Yes, I'm the kid who threw up on your shoe," I say, his forgetfulness stinging in a way I didn't expect. "I'll go home now. I can catch the bus. I'm just going to get Meridee...."

"She's not going anywhere and neither are you." He takes a step toward me, and I put my hands up.

"Don't!"

"I'm not going to hurt you; you just can't go out in the night. And she lives here. Sit down or at least calm down. Jesus." He rubs his chin more fiercely, the pressure moving the wrinkled skin on his face. "I remember you now, just took me a minute."

"What's my name?"

He hesitates. "Something with a *p*: Patty?"

I don't bother to give him my real name.

"Sorry, but my brain's pretty fuzzy. I was drinking a lot back then. Janet had lost the twins, and she wasn't getting out of bed. I thought having another kid would help. I thought it might…Shoulda known it'd be like getting a kid a dog. They say they'll take care of it, but it ends up being you doin' all the walks and feedin' it. I wasn't prepared to be a dad to the twins, and I sure wasn't prepared to take care of some stranger's kid."

I stare at him, this man folding inward like a crushed aluminum can. He sits down at the table across from me.

"I didn't think we'd ever want to foster a kid again after you left, but then last year she took all the baby clothes and stuff to her church. Wanted to go back to those foster parent classes. I stopped fighting the dogs a couple of years ago, just kept them all eating and howling out there. Then we got Ms. Meridee...."

At the sound of her name, Meridee enters the kitchen. "Poppa N, can Pavi and I have popcorn?"

She's like an angel sweeping light into the room. Now I can see she's wearing a new pair of purple Barbie pajamas. Her braids aren't as neat as when I last saw her, but I doubt Mr. Nickerson knows anything about doing her hair. When she smiles, I notice she's lost one of her bottom teeth. Mr. Nickerson's face softens as he reaches out a hand to her. She takes it, and he pulls her up onto his lap. Her hands clamp around his whiskered chin, and he pretends to chomp her fingers, the two of them laughing together.

"I got popcorn in the living room."

"Is it burnt?" Meridee asks, her eyebrows skeptical.

"Probably."

"Poppa N! Why you burnin' it every day?"

He smiles. "I like it burnt."

He pushes her off his lap. "You go eat some popcorn in the living room while Pavi calls her family. It's late, and she needs to get her head checked out."

We both watch Meridee walk into the living room on her tiptoes, then hear an aggressive knock at the door. Before Mr. Nickerson can cross the kitchen, we hear the swing of the door opening and Meridee's voice.

"Poppa N, the polices are here!"

I race to the living room to see two officers standing in the doorway, and behind them, her arms outstretched, is Marjorie.

# TELLING MARJORIE THE TRUTH

Marjorie and I sit crammed together on the front step, our bodies tight between the narrow metal railings. The tips of my shoelaces dip into the slats of the wooden steps, bobbing up and down with the tap of my foot, like a fishing line waiting for a bite. Inside, the police are talking to Mr. Nickerson, probably at the kitchen table where he and I were sitting moments before. They'll talk to me next, but Marjorie wanted to see me first, to get me outside the house so I could breathe normally.

"Where's Hamilton?" I ask, my eyes on my shoes.

"In the car."

"And Piper?"

"She's in the car, too; her parents are on the way."

I groan, thinking about all the people who are involved now: police officers and parents, soon the case-workers at Crossroads, and…I wonder if Santos's foster mom will come. I wonder if he's still here, though I can't picture him shivering in the back of Marjorie's station wagon while Piper films a testimonial of her near-death experience. I don't know how to ask Marjorie so that she won't suspect he was here. I don't want to get him involved if I don't have to.

"Are they both okay?"

Marjorie nods. "I'll have to take Hamilton in to make sure he doesn't need stitches, but it doesn't look very deep. Piper is…overstimulated, but she should calm down soon."

"I'm really sorry I got them both into this," I say, realizing I am sorry. Hamilton could have been home practicing his baritone, but instead he's in the back of a station wagon bleeding all over the seat. Stitches.

My head throbs, and I lie my head down on my lap, crossing my arms under my cheek. Marjorie's hand rubs swirls along my back, her fingers occasionally curling to make a sunburst shape, fireworks along my spine. Now I know why Hamilton begs his mom for a back rub sometimes. It's soothing, like waves to ease my breaths, and I think I will finally answer all the questions she has yet to ask.

"We didn't come to break in. We came to save that little girl, Meridee."

"Is she in danger?" Marjorie's eyebrows furrow, and I pause because I don't know anymore. Just an hour ago, I was certain her whole life was falling apart, and then there was the teddy bear and Poppa N and it doesn't make sense anymore why we are here, sitting on his front step with the police inside.

"I don't think so. Not anymore."

"Can you tell me why you thought she was in danger? Enough danger that you would risk your own life to come get her?"

"We weren't going to kidnap her. We were just gathering evidence."

"Evidence?"

"Do you hear the dogs in the backyard?"

Marjorie nods.

"It started with the dogs...." I take a breath and let the memories I've been holding back flood out of me like a broken dam. I tell her everything about the dogs, the loneliness, Lucky.

"Oh, Pavi," Marjorie says, pulling me tight to her body, and I claw my way out of the past by describing my present. Marjorie smells like a rose. My shoelaces are untied. "That's awful. I'm sorry about your puppy, and I'm sorry you had to be around such terrible behavior."

"But I don't understand," I say. "I got here and the dogs were just in their cages and there was a teddy bear on the floor. He's supposed to be a bad guy, but he gave her a teddy bear."

Marjorie rubs her hand over my hair. "It sounds like he's a very different man now than he was when you were here. He didn't know how to be a good guardian to you. Or to his dogs."

"But it's not just him!" I shout, pulling myself out of her grasp. "It's my mom, too! I did everything she wanted me to! I never cried in front of her, and I found us dinner when she couldn't, and I got good grades on my report cards, and waited for her to come back, but none of it mattered."

Something in me breaks, like the snapping of branches in a windstorm, and I feel myself slowly collapsing, no more support beams to hold me up.

"I don't think I'm ever going to see my mom again."

Marjorie reaches out to grab my hands. She pulls me toward her, my head resting on her shoulder, her cheek pressed against my hair. "I'm so sorry, sweetie. I'm sorry your mom doesn't get to see how wonderful you are."

She pushes me back so she can look at me, placing her hands around my cheeks.

"You are an incredible girl. You are kind and smart and funny and brave. So brave that you would come back to such a scary place to try and save someone else. You're a hero, Pavi."

Marjorie tilts her head so she can look right into my eyes.

"But you wouldn't have to do any of that. I love you and Hambone loves you, just for you. Without you doing anything at all. It's a shame that people like Mr. Nickerson couldn't see that."

I sniffle, rubbing my sleeve under my nose to prevent the drips. The door creaks.

"Excuse me, ma'am, can we speak to you inside?" The young officer looks sympathetic as Marjorie helps me to my feet. "Shouldn't take long. I know you want to get your kids home."

He pushes the door open wider to accommodate the two of us, since Marjorie still has me tucked under her arm. As we step toward the door, I glance across the street and there he is, Santos, resting against the telephone pole at the end of the block. When our eyes connect, he nods. Then he turns and heads off down the dark street.

# THE END

When I get to the stairs, Santos is sitting on the cement ledge, his backpack beside him, an open bag of Hot Cheetos on his lap. Around him swirl students heading home, some in packs, some alone, some ready to bolt from the school grounds, and others wishing they could stay at school a little longer, eat one more meal, have one more person ask about their day. It's his one-month check-in even though we talk almost every day. His foster mom let him finish out the grading period here, but his school transfer finally goes through next week, and then we won't see each other anymore. At least not until his six-month appointment.

He pulls out his headphones when he sees me

climbing the stairs. He grabs a handful of Cheetos and tosses them in his mouth, his head tilted back like he's a sword-swallower preparing for a performance.

"That better not be my payment you're eating," I say, hopping on the ledge beside him.

"Nah," he says as he unzips his backpack, pulling out a family size bag of Hot Cheetos and two packs of multicolored Sharpies. There's even a set of the metallic Sharpies, which are never on sale.

"You only owed me the Cheetos and a four-pack of Sharpies." I hold the rainbow twenty-four-pack, imagining the work I can do to the plain lunch box Marjorie bought me last week.

"You can have them."

I don't argue and shove the supplies in my backpack. I grab the manila folder with his name on it, reviewing the research I originally did on his foster mom and his one-week check-in form. I skim over his grade reports and some notes I took after our first meetings. "Doesn't seem to want services," I wrote, and beside that a frowny face and "Those earbuds." Out of my general folder I pull the one-month form and hand it to him on a clipboard.

"Fill out the top portion; it's a basic survey. If nothing much has changed at home—which it sounds like it hasn't—then it should be pretty easy. We'll talk new-school information when you're finished."

He nods, grabbing a pen from his back pocket. He pulls the cap off with his teeth and continues to hold the lid in his mouth, crunching the edge as he writes.

"Meridee is going back with her family," I say, and he turns, the faintest hint of a smile on his lips. "Not to her mom yet, but to an aunt in Georgia. The Crossroads staff wouldn't tell me more than that."

No one there talks to me the same way anymore, not since they learned about the break-in at the Nickersons'. I haven't seen Lenny since he came to school to question me, but I hope he'll see the situation like I do: We were just trying to save her. I hate that he doesn't trust me, and my business really needs him, especially since Hamilton and I will be meeting a new client at Crossroads today.

"She's going home," Santos says, and I pause.

"Maybe…"

Because what is home for us foster kids? We don't have one place to grow up, a bedroom that holds a crib, then a twin bed, then bunk beds, finally ending with a full-size mattress, or, if we're lucky, a queen. We don't get to choose the paint colors that change around us as we grow. You can't measure us along the wall, tracking our lives with pencil marks and dates the way Marjorie keeps track of Hamilton on the kitchen doorframe. Will her aunt's house be home? I don't know. I hope it's home enough. That it has enough love to at least be more than a house.

"We're having a going-away party for her at Crossroads today if you want to come. Hamilton is meeting me here as soon as we're finished so we can walk over." Meridee's been back at Crossroads since right after we broke in because the Nickersons aren't verified foster parents anymore. The police discovered the dogs, and even though they weren't fighting anymore, her caseworker decided they were too dangerous, given their history.

"I can't today; tell her bye." Santos checks one more box. "Done."

I reach for a handful of Cheetos before taking it from him and scanning his answers. "I'm glad Ms. Graves is going so well."

"She asks a lot of questions. She makes pie."

I wonder if she'll ever get to hear him say that. Probably not. But maybe she can tell the small things he does that let her know he doesn't hate her guts. Maybe she notices the earbuds aren't always in, too. I hand him my New School FAQ packet.

"This has all the information you need to get started

next week. I checked in with my contacts at Webb and put down the names of the good counselor, and a teacher, Ms. Black, who's supposed to be cool with foster kids, and the names of some classes you definitely want to take. If you send me your student cloud log-in, I can run you a few reports on your grades and credits. The school is supposed to send it over, but it's better to have your own copy. You don't want to end up in PE again, or back in seventh grade."

"Cool."

He takes the packet and rolls it into a tube before stuffing it into his hoodie pocket.

"That's all I have for now. We'll check in again in six months. Hopefully it will still be all good."

"I'll see you tomorrow at lunch?" He slides his earbuds back into his ears.

"Yeah, tomorrow at lunch."

He nods before hopping off the ledge. "Bye, Pav."

I smile at the nickname as he takes off across the street. As I stuff the Sharpies and Hot Cheetos in my backpack, I hear Hamilton calling my name.

~

When we get to Crossroads, Lenny is sitting at the front desk. We have a face-off moment, then he smiles.

"Pavi Sharma. Superstar," he says as I walk toward the counter. "Honor roll, perfect attendance, rescuer of children…" His voice softens as he reaches out to fist-bump. "Sorry I didn't believe you, Pav."

I shrug, not sure what to say. *I'm sorry you didn't, too. There would have been fewer stitches if you had.*

"Sorry I almost got her hospitalized with fake appendicitis."

He laughs. "Wait. That's why you taught her that game? Geez, Pav, you're like an evil genius. Well, not evil. Just genius."

I can feel my cheeks starting to turn red.

"I assume you're here for the party?"

"Yep." And to meet a new client, but he doesn't need to know about that.

"And you're the partner in crime," Lenny says, leaning over to give Hamilton a fist bump, too.

*And in business,* I think as Hamilton and I share a smile. Right now he's helping me with my clients, but we're brainstorming something new: Hamilton helping biological kids adjust to their new foster siblings. The two of us taking on foster care from both sides. This way he can earn his own Hot Cheetos. He's become an addict. His fingertips are going to be permanently stained red.

"You two save me a slice of cake," Lenny says, giving me one last fist bump.

In the den, we find Piper surrounded by a group of kids at folding tables. A few days after the break-in, she asked me how she could help out other foster kids like Meridee, and while I don't trust her with my business, I knew her makeup skills could go to good use. Now a couple of times a month, she helps with the Heart Gallery photo shoots for foster kids hoping to be adopted. No goths or merpeople, but she does help kids waiting for forever families look their best. She and I won't be best friends (it will take a long time to forget all the awful things she's said), but I appreciate that she's trying to think about someone other than herself. And she is pretty good at makeovers.

Hamilton and I sit down at the tables. Piper looks up from where she is adding blush to the freckled cheek of a young boy I believe is our new client, James. He's the only one in the room I haven't worked with yet.

"Looks good, Pipe," Hamilton says as he plays with a cotton ball on the table.

"Thanks," she says, scanning her supplies. "Pavi, can you hand me that lip balm?"

I search the mounds of materials on the table before finding a tub full of different types of lip balms.

"Which one?" I hold up three different shades of pink. Piper turns to the boy. "Which one do you like?"

"Do you have a sparkly one?" he asks, his voice barely above a whisper.

"This one has all the sparkles," Piper says as she plucks one of the tubes from my hand.

"Are you James?" I ask him before realizing he can't answer with his mouth puckered.

He nods.

"Nice to meet you. I'm Pavi, and this is Hamilton. We're here to talk to you about your new family. Alexa told you about us?" He rubs his eyes. I hope Hamilton and I aren't intimidating, so I try to talk softer. "We can talk when you're finished getting ready. You probably have a while before they take your pictures."

I grab the intake forms out of my bag. "Hamilton, you can start with James while I talk to Meridee. I want a few minutes alone before the party starts."

"Sure thing," he says, taking the papers from my hand.

I find Meridee in the backyard, holding the teddy bear I saw that night at the Nickersons', but it has the sock I gave her pulled over its head like an elf hat. She's humming the high-pitched melody of a classroom song, one her teachers probably taught her.

"What are you singing?" I ask as I sit across from her in the grass.

"It's the seat song," she says, clapping the bear's paws together as she sings. "Everybody have a seat, have a seat. Everybody have a seat, a seat on the floor. Not on the ceiling, not on the door, a seat on the floor."

I give her and the teddy a round of applause.

"So you're going to see your auntie in Georgia?" I ask, pulling the sock-hat lower on the teddy bear's head.

"Auntie Trish."

"That sounds fun!"

"I'm going to see Mama at Auntie Trish's."

I pause. I don't think that's true. "Did someone tell you that you were going to see Mama?"

"Sometimes she talks to Auntie Trish on the phone, and Mama asks her to send us some money."

I reach for her, pulling her into my lap. "Sometimes mamas can't come to live with us, even if we are the best kids of all. Sometimes mamas are sick, or they have to work too much, or sometimes they forget how to be mamas, and so their little girls have to go live with someone new."

"Did your mama forget how to be a mama?" Mer-idee looks back at me, pressing a palm to my cheek.

"She did, and so now I live with a new family, with Hambone...."

"Hambone!"

"Yes, with Hambone and Marjorie, and she's like a mama." I take Meridee's hands between mine, rocking us side to side in the grass. "So, Auntie Trish is going to be like a mama for you. And maybe your mama will remember how to take good care of you, and maybe she will just stay sick, but you will always have someone who loves you."

"Hambone loves me!"

"He does."

"And you love me!"

"I do."

I spin her around so she is facing me on the grass. "I have one more game to teach you before you go, okay?"

She nods, then scoops up her teddy and gives it a smooch on the nose. Knowing there will be no Hot Cheetos or school supplies or any payment on the way, I start lesson one.

"This game is called Front Door Face. Want to try?"

As I begin lesson one, I know I'll teach her what I can. Even if she doesn't learn it all, I know she will survive.

## ACKNOWLEDGMENTS

Thank you to my editor, Nikki Garcia, for loving Pavi, Hamilton, Santos—and even Piper—from the very beginning. You made the story tighter and suggested fixes to problems I knew existed but hadn't yet solved, all while keeping the characters the same at heart. Marisa Finkelstein, Marcie Lawrence, Katharine Mc-Anarney, Stefanie Hoffman, Bill Grace, Jennifer Poe, and everyone at Little, Brown Books for Young Readers whose talent and creativity gave Pavi a life beyond what I had imagined, thank you for helping to tell this story.

To my agent, Melissa Edwards. From our very first phone call in my classroom, you've made a process that seemed so difficult and impenetrable suddenly easy and accessible. Your technical expertise gave me space to just write. Thank you.

To my book coach, Resa Alboher. You helped shape Pavi, Hamilton, and the crew. Thank you for brainstorming their world and their lives. And to Justine Duhr, owner of WritebyNight, for providing the book coaching services without which I couldn't have published this novel. Thank you for allowing me flexibility in services and for sharing your publishing savvy.

To Addie Alexander, for your social work expertise and the idea of appendicitis. Thank you also to my sensitivity readers, including Sally Fussell of SAFE Foster and Adopt, Idris Grey, and Rudy Ramirez, for allowing me to see the story in new ways and helping me assure a respectful representation for all kids who read it. I'm grateful for your support in shaping Pavi's perspective as one outside my own experience.

Thank you to Aaron Lindstrom, for sharing your experience with adoption and the challenges of having parents who don't look like you. To Britta Lundin, for answering my many panicked texts throughout the writing and publishing process. I often feel like your geeky little sister and am so grateful to be able to follow in your footsteps. To Patrick Cook, who I first shared this idea with over six years ago, thank you for not liking everything I do just because we're friends. And to Travis Bedard, my mentor for all things literary and theatrical.

Thank you to the many readers and brainstorming

partners who've read drafts, given feedback on titles, or compiled middle school slang. Such wonderful people include Ria, the film meet-up crew (Alison, Jo, and Tony), Lara, Nina, Elizabeth, Emily, and my new book coach Jessamine Chan. A special thank-you to my first student reader, Connor, for his detailed feedback and continuous excitement.

To my sisters, Sara and Ashley, who built my imagination through hay-loft homes at Grandma Dee's and stake-outs of stuffed-animal-poaching bad guys whispering through the air vents. I'm forever grateful to my parents for reading my notebooks full of novels about World War II and the *Titanic*. Thank you, Mom, for binding my first story about mermaids with that peach, seashell wallpaper. You both believed I was a writer before it was official.

And finally, to Shiva. You may not have started your own consulting agency for other foster kids, but we all know you could have. This story—this wonderful life— would not exist without you. I love you forever.